A COLLECTOR'S ITEM

The Cobbler's Last

Mollee Kruger . . . earns the Gold Standard for the most insightful, historically valuable, skillfully written, and entertaining memoir by a county resident.

Jim Chrismer, author and Harford County, Maryland, historian

Told with compassion and wit . . . fascinating details skillfully woven into the narrative.

Vonnie Crist, *Harford's Heart*

Reminds elder readers of simpler times and offers younger readers perspective on surviving tough economic times.

Brooke Kenny, *The Gazette*

Strong and compassionate understanding of what it's like to be parent or child . . . gives a great sense of the world my parents grew up in.

Marshall Brinn, author

The Swift Seasons

The infirm, lonely and forgotten . . . An inside look into a world . . . that shadows our society obsessively focused on the culture of youth.

Washington Beacon

If you have an eighty-year-old in your life, this is an illuminating, enchanting read.

Mitali Perkins, author, *Rickshaw Girl* and *Monsoon Summer*

One of the surprises of the book is how funny it is. All the same, [it] moved me as few novels had . . . wonderful and profound.

Noah Efron, author

A clever, insightful book. The light verse and the somber notes are worth a read in and of themselves.

Bill Slott, author and travel consultant

Much wisdom in Kruger's wonderful book . . . How to live with dignity and what we may expect after our eightieth birthday.

Alon Tal, author

Port of Call

Long awaited, often humorous, sequel to *The Cobbler's Last* . . . focuses on the many distractions that can keep authors from reaching their metaphorical ports of call.

Emily Tipermas, *Lifetimes*, Charles E. Smith Life Communities

Kosher Salt

A mix of serious subjects and lighthearted fun.

Lauren Rosenblatt, *Pittsburgh Jewish Chronicle*

A Purse of Verse for the Jewish Woman

Feminist views about biblical women, cleverly comparing them to modern-day characters . . . tenderly poking fun at the female gender.

Sara Trappler Spielman, *Hadassah Magazine*

Full of light sardonic rhymes which reflect . . . topics familiar to today's woman.

Nancy Slavin, Public TV producer

Historical humor and wit . . . a delightfully entertaining and educational purse of verse.

Stanley Barkan, poet and editor, *Cross-Cultural Communications*

Ladies First

Witty Ogden Nash-like . . . focuses on the love-hate relationship between voters and presidents' wives. Clever candle-lighting history with a girlish glow.

Nick DiSpoldo, *Small Press Review*

With her light touch and contagious humor, the poet gives us an insightful lesson in American history. Mollee Kruger's guided tour of the White House is a tour de force.

Marta Knobloch, *The Pen Woman*

Yankee Shoes

Written with a Bicentennial flavor, the collection of more than eighty short folk poems and ballads . . . reflects an American perspective on love, war, marriage, and politics from one hundred years ago to the present.

Washington Jewish Week

Admiral of the Mosquitos

Literary excursion into history. Light and humorous poems . . . might make you think of the zany couplets of Gilbert and Sullivan.

Leonard Hughes, *Washington Post*

A gentle lament for Columbus . . . an indictment of Queen Isabella.

Samuel Goldreich, *Baltimore Sun*

Chucklesome writing . . . a combination of Dorothy Parker and Carl Sandburg. Jolly poetry here . . . a rollicking romp through history.

The Book Reader

Unholy Writ and More Unholy Writ

She possesses wit, facile use of satire, a good eye and ear for rhyme and rhythm, and ease of expression.

In Jewish Bookland

A deft sense of humor . . . Kruger has done for her "proud, stiff-necked people" what Pulitzer Prize winner Phyllis McGinley did for St. Teresa.

Pittsburgh Jewish Chronicle

A sharp philosophical eye . . . will cause readers to say, "Gee, I wish I'd said that!" or "How true!"

Cleveland Jewish News

A COLLECTOR'S ITEM

Novella, short stories, and selected essays

Mollee Kruger

A MARYBEN BOOK

Kruger, Mollee
A Collector's Item

1. Aging 2. Friendship 3. Retirement 4. Covid-19
5. Humor 6. Journalism 7. Small towns 8. Jewish Americans

ISBN: 978-09912289-4-2 (paperback)
ISBN: 978-09912289-5-9 (e-book)
Library of Congress Control Number: 22022906812
LCCN Imprint: Rockville, MD

Design: Carolyn K. Lewis, www.cklewis.com
Cover image: Carolyn K. Lewis

Printed in the United States of America

To all those who are too young to be old and too old to be young

CONTENTS

THE NOVELLA

A COLLECTOR'S ITEM

"What did you say, Marie-Elana? Wait, let me turn up my hearing aid." Deborah adjusted the white knob in her ear.

"I throw the garbage away." The young housekeeper switched off the vacuum cleaner. A thick purple scarf covered her mouth and nose.

The old woman couldn't believe what she heard. "Excuse me. You did what?"

"I throw it out, that mess," Marie-Elana yelled, and then shook her head as if she couldn't understand such a big commotion over a piece of trash.

Keep calm, Deborah told herself. Just yesterday on the public address system Ms. Patel, the in-house social worker, urged tenants to be patient and understanding. "All personnel vacancies will be filled as soon as possible," she said. But she didn't tell them outright that maintenance people didn't care to work at a place where the elderly residents couldn't always remember to wash their hands, keep their distance, or wear masks.

"You should have asked my permission first." Deborah spoke as gently as she could. During her years as a teacher, she had always prided herself on self-control no matter what chaos was going on around her. She did sympathize with the overworked housekeepers. But still.

"Marie-Elana, that was a valuable magazine," Deborah said. Now she could feel her blood pressure soaring. Her voice rose with each word. "Can't you get it back?"

"You mean pick through garbage?"

"Yes, if that's necessary. I—I could help." Deborah felt herself fighting back tears.

"The lady in charge she told us don't be touching too much dirty stuff," Marie-Elana said, wiggling her gloved fingers for emphasis. "Get sick that way."

"But I need it," Deborah said. "I need that magazine." Her voice broke. "I meant to show it to Sally."

Marie-Elana answered by turning on the vacuum cleaner full blast.

That evening a newly hired waiter brought dinner to the apartment. "No more eat in the dining room," said the immigrant Black man. He pushed a gurney loaded with plastic containers of Caribbean-style chicken stew and collard greens. "Everybody keep away from everybody now," he said, fiddling with a flimsy mask that kept sliding down his nose.

All through dinner at her wobbly TV table, Deborah couldn't concentrate on watching the evening news about the pandemic. She spent the hours before bedtime trying to understand why Marie-Elana had considered The Magazine worthless. Certainly, the outdated periodical wasn't a thing of beauty, permanently curled in half, bent at an arthritic angle, the jagged pages fluted with brown. The elderly woman could vaguely remember a long-ago thunderstorm when she had rescued The Magazine, sopping wet, from the cellar of her home. The pages dried out, but they were never the same again.

"Paper and people can assume new identities," her friend Sally once wrote in one of her New Age articles. "Texture changes over the years."

Late into the night Deborah Greenbaum lay awake in bed as she often did, remembering, pushing away all that should have been forgotten by now. Old people don't sleep well at night, she lectured herself; it will pass. She should have complained to the management about what Marie-Elana did with The Magazine. Sally would have thrown a tantrum.

Don't get started again, she told herself, as she lifted her head and squinted to read the ghostly digital numbers on her bedside clock. Midnight. Stop it. You'll be a wreck in the morning. But Sally gave no ground. She refused to disappear, all the wild things she did, all the brave, outrageous things. Deborah closed her eyes, and an army of memories confronted her, infiltrating her sleep.

1948

"Looks like we have bunk beds," the girl with the fiery red hair said. She dropped a heavy suitcase onto the uncarpeted floor. "You get the lower one."

"No," Deborah said in her timid voice. "That's okay. I'll take the upper."

"But you were here first."

"Only by a half hour."

"Suits me." The stranger tossed a blue checkered blanket onto the narrow bed. "Hey," she said. "I'm going to nominate you for Best Freshman Roommate of all time." She offered her hand. "You must be Deborah. I'm Sally. My dad was in the Navy, and we lived all over. I tell people I'm from Everywhere."

"I come from Boxton over in Montrovia County," Deborah said. She had wanted to answer with a joke like, "I'm from Nowhere," but her new roommate might think she was making fun of her. They unpacked in silence. Deborah hoped she wouldn't have to go into her own background with a boring rigamarole about her aunt's dress shop on Main Street. That would hardly impress a worldly type like Sally.

The two freshman girls at State U. had been assigned to a room in a dormitory that once housed boys. The historic campus had changed. There was hardly enough room to accommodate the high enrollment of both sexes. Wooden annexations sprouted throughout the university. The Administration found itself woefully unprepared to handle the masses of young men home from a world war they never talked about.

"Ten guys for every girl," Sally noted during Orientation Week. "We should kneel down and give thanks for the Bountiful Season of the G.I. Bill." Deborah agreed although not cleverly. "Right," she said.

They walked slowly, their arms laden with textbooks from the campus bookstore. "It's hard to find my way around," Deborah said. "I keep getting lost."

"Whatever you do, don't follow the crowd," Sally said, "which I actually did today in Cameron Hall, and walked right into the men's john." She laughed. "It's one way to meet men if you're looking for a MRS. degree."

"Which I'm not," Deborah said.

Sally was intrigued that their bathrooms had retained urinals used by the former residents. During Freshman Week she sent a personal letter to the Dean of Women, Dr. Amirantha Rutherford.

"Here's a suggestion for utilizing the masculine toilets in our dorm," Sally wrote. "Why don't we plant geraniums in them?" Dean Rutherford was known as "Miss Priss" to her young ladies. She replied to Sally's suggestion with a hand-printed reprimand on note paper embossed with the official State seal: "Your comment, young woman," she wrote, "is in wretchedly poor taste. Please learn to be more discreet." Sally howled with delight.

That was Sally. Beautiful Sally. She smoked Chesterfields before breakfast. She played bridge half the night with other teenage night owls. She muted her alarm clock by wrapping it in a thick towel, buried it in her dresser drawer, and laughed when she overslept her eight o'clock class the next morning. But this wasn't the worst as Deborah was soon to discover. On the roadway below the dorm windows, a tall streetlight illuminated their room all night long like a lighthouse beacon.

"I can fix this. Step outside with me," Sally said one autumnal evening when it began to get dark early. By the side of the gravel road that ran past the building, Sally found a rock. She took careful aim, hurled it, and cheered YAY! as broken glass tumbled to the ground. The nocturnal brightness disappeared from their room, and they could sleep at last. Repair came slowly. When it did, Deborah cringed to see Sally tossing rocks again and again until the maintenance men stopped coming.

Although horrified at first, Deborah never protested. Deep down, she took vicarious pleasure in her roommate's runaway chutzpah. In sophomore year, when Sally's parents refused to give their free-wheeling daughter additional spending money, she went into business, collecting dirty sweaters, skirts, and jackets from other girls in the dorm. Each week she carried heavy loads of woolens to the local dry cleaner's, a convenient service for those who could afford her fee.

Deborah disliked the soiled clothing of strangers littering all corners of their room, but when Sally asked, "Do you mind?" Deborah answered, "No, it's fine."

"Ever notice there aren't any vending machines in this creaky old building?" Sally observed the following week. "We could buy candy bars at the drugstore and sell them here at a profit. How about it?"

Deborah couldn't bring herself to protest. "We'd have to stay in the room all day, wouldn't we, to keep an eye on things?" Perhaps she could provide a logical response without having to be outright disagreeable. She had read somewhere that Jews often answer questions with questions.

"The honor system. They come in, take what they want, and leave the money. What do you think, Deb?"

Deborah supplied the only answer that would make her roommate happy: "If that's what you want to do." Above all, she didn't dare to cross her only friend on campus. Over the lifetime that followed, she would lie awake at night, posing the ambiguous question: "What did I do to deserve Sally Anne Harrigan?"

1951

By their junior year, Sally had abandoned the world of small business and dedicated herself to the greater good of mankind. As managing editor of the *Weekly Horizon*, the campus newspaper, she planned to run a series of articles about a decaying Negro college in a remote part of the state. She insisted that Deborah cut classes and join her on a long bus ride past abandoned mills and rundown farms to Freeman Regional Academy. Compared to their own state university, they found the segregated college to be substandard. The halls of the Arts and Sciences building were unheated and dark, and class members shared a scant number of textbooks. The overhead lighting was dim and the ventilation poor. Some students took notes on pads of brown paper cut from grocery bags.

"Separate but equal, my foot," Sally said on the ride home. "Didn't we win a war to ensure the Four Freedoms? Well, there ought to be a Fifth one: Freedom to Get a Decent Education." With Deborah assigned to researching background material, Sally planned to expose the Jim Crow situation in three articles for the campus newspaper. Deborah thought they were playing with fire, but she couldn't say no to Sally.

They had hardly finished the project when Deborah's worst nightmare came true. "Old Miss Priss wants to see me in her office tomorrow," Sally said. "Someone spilled the beans. She's afraid we're engaged in subversive activity. Doesn't that turn your stomach?"

Deborah felt like saying, I told you so, or even better, Why not quit and let well enough alone? But if she objected, maybe her roommate would disown her. And it would be a disaster for a clumsy, fat-faced nothing from Nowhere to lose an incomparable treasure like Sally.

"I'm not advocating anything radical, although I'm tempted," Sally continued. "We're just being realistic. Why does everybody turn so yellow when it comes to telling the truth?"

Deborah shrugged. "The sign of the times," she answered, but she wanted to warn Sally to stay in the good graces of the bigwigs. It was not the first time Sally had crossed Dean Rutherford. "She detests me anyway," Sally said. "Look at this royal summons she sent."

Deborah shrank from even touching the letter. "No, I believe you," she said.

"Stop shaking in your boots. You don't have to come with me. She wants my rear end on a platter, but in a way, I'm lucky."

"How?"

"Because girls don't get to be top dog around these parts. The buck stops with our hard-drinking-till-he's-stinking Predator-in-Chief."

"Maybe they'll kick us out and Bill Hadley too."

"No, it's okay. Bill promised he'd back us up. I've dated him a few times. He's a war hero, Bronze Star, bless him. Goes bananas when he thinks freedom of the press is in danger. Anyway, he has an appointment tomorrow with Dr. Sutton."

Deborah shook her head. All was lost. If the State U. president knew about it, he could expel the whole bunch, and how would she explain it to her Aunt Tziporah? There would be hell to pay.

"Cheer up, Deb. Bill can fast-talk anybody. That's what an editor-in-chief does. Don't look so worried."

It didn't go well. "They read him the riot act. Literally," Sally said. "And, good for him, Bill exchanged words with both Sutton and that jerk, what-sis-name, the Dean of Men. They think our series is Commie propaganda aimed at desegregating the whole rotten education system in this state. And the hilarious thing is, they haven't read a word of it yet."

"We're in big trouble," Deborah said.

"Let me finish. So then afterward, Bill said, and I quote him verbatim, 'To hell with that bunch of bigots. Let's go with it. Just water it down a bit.'"

Deborah felt the corners of her mouth sag. "How?"

"Bill decided we should make it less explosive, use the passive voice lots more, run it as a single article, not a whole series. I want you to find me some complicated quotes to make it look scholarly. Like a term paper. Go heavy on the footnotes. We'll even quote some palaver from official university brochures. If it's camouflaged, nice and bland, we can still print the truth and get away with it."

Why did I ever get mixed up in something like this, Deborah asked herself. She stayed up late for an entire week working on the revision with Sally and prayed that Bill would decide at the last minute not to use any of it. If Aunt Tziporah found out, she would have conniptions.

The *Weekly Horizon* printed it under the headline, "The Idea of a University?," borrowed, Sally explained, from the Catholic theologian John Cardinal Newman.

"Look, the sky didn't fall," Sally said after the article appeared. "A few Army veterans agreed with it, but most of the student body never bothered to read it. Talk about apathy!"

Yes, Deborah thought, but what about the alumni association, the governor's office, and the state legislature? Wouldn't they find out and raise the roof? She kept these questions to herself.

Bill escaped with a severe reprimand, and the Dean of Women enjoyed her revenge. "I hear she's responsible for blackballing me," Sally said when she learned she had not been tapped by a national women's honorary society for leadership and scholarship. Deborah knew the punishment hurt Sally, who bravely responded with, "I'll consider it a badge of honor for the rest of my life."

At the end of senior year, Sally made a serious announcement. "I've decided," she told Deborah, "we have the magic touch working together, you researching, me writing. We ought to tackle serious careers in journalism."

"Okay," Deborah said, but deep down she asked herself, why? I'm not Sally.

"So we won't move to New York right away, Deb. Before settling down to the nitty-gritty of job hunting, we give Paris a chance. If it was good enough for Hemingway and Fitzgerald, it's the only place in the world for you and me at this stage of the game."

"Sounds good," Deborah said in a small voice. Sally had such crazy ideas. It was best to humor her and let it all fade away in time.

But Sally persisted, growing more and more determined as graduation day approached. "If we work hard at summer jobs waiting tables and borrow a little here and there, we'll get to France by late September."

"That's only months away."

Sally had it all planned. "First we'll do serious research on modern French culture. We should study expat memoirs. Hey, know what? I just found a paperback called *Paris on Five Dollars a Day*." Sally was almost dancing with excitement. "As soon as we get there, we'll rent a flat in the middle of Montmartre where all the action is. And with my French minor, won't that be wild?"

Deborah went along with what she imagined was Sally's fantasy. But when her friend began dialing airlines about actual reservations, that was sheer recklessness. It was time to work up enough nerve to speak out. She tried to sound casual. "Let's not do anything foolish we'll regret, Sally."

"What do you mean? You and I will be the toast of Paree."

"My Aunt Tziporah always says, 'Talking is one thing. Doing is something else.'"

"What's gotten into you, Deb? Are you sick?"

Deborah felt her head spinning, but for once, she spoke as fast as she could manage. "This year I switched from Liberal Arts to the College of Education."

"You never told me that."

"I'm sorry."

"You collected education credits on the sly, and I never even knew about it?"

Deborah avoided eye contact. "I guess you've been busy with meeting deadlines for the *Weekly Horizon*. Anyway, our last six weeks of this semester, I'll be practice teaching."

Sally took a deep breath. "Why on earth would you do that?"

"I heard there's an opening this fall at Grammbly Elementary School. It's down the street from where my aunt and I live. I've already applied for it. With a degree in primary education, my chances are good."

"You mean you'd give up Europe now just to teach a bunch of snot-nosed little kids?"

"I can live at home and help out with expenses. My aunt owns a dress shop, but she's not well and wants to sell it one of these days."

"What about all our plans?"

Tears welled up in Deborah's eyes. "I can't go with you, Sally. I'd be lost there. It's all too scary for me."

"Scary? It'll be fun."

"Anyway, that's not something I really want to do."

Sally remained silent for a long time. "I'm flying to Paris," she said with a sense of finality, "with or without you." She shook her head. "Really, Deb, I thought you had more spirit."

Deborah didn't answer. She had always depended upon the guidance of her Aunt Tziporah, who disapproved of frivolous behavior that wasted time and money. She was quick-tempered but kind in her own Old Country way, devoted to her orphaned niece. The time had come for repayment. It would be cruel to consider abandoning her.

After four years together, Deborah felt worn down by Sally's exhausting spontaneity. Deborah was convinced of one thing. Although creative and dynamic, although smart and aggressive, although charming and beautiful, live-wire Sally lacked one basic human trait: common sense.

Still, in the years ahead, neither of them would display superior wisdom when it came to choosing the men in their lives.

1954

On a cold morning when the sidewalks of Boxton were treacherous from a recent ice storm, Deborah in her lined galoshes walked gingerly from the post office to Grammbly Elementary School. She carried a letter in her handbag. The long envelope bore the words "Par Avion." It was the first time she had ever received correspondence from someone who didn't live in the United States, and she wanted to share the excitement with her first graders.

"Look, class," she said as soon as the children finished reciting the Lord's Prayer and the Pledge of Allegiance, "this is a letter sent all the way from Paris. That's a city far, far away across the Atlantic Ocean in a beautiful country called France. Isn't this a pretty red French stamp?"

"Yes ma'am," her class said in unison.

"I'll pass the envelope around so you all can see it."

A little girl with tight corkscrew curls raised her hand.

"Yes, Mildred?"

"What does the letter say?"

"Many, many things that only grown-ups would understand." Deborah smiled broadly. The contents weren't suitable for six-year-olds, and she certainly wasn't about to read it for the class. At recess she savored the message on the tissue-thin paper one more time to make sure she hadn't missed anything important.

Hey Deb,

You haven't heard from me because I haven't had a permanent address. I am now living in St.-Germain-des-Prés with a divine bearded Frenchman, one Henri Romaine, a classically trained violist. From him, I am learning to appreciate the work of composers we never heard of at State U., geniuses like Milhaud and Honegger. He teaches me an abundance of Other Things, but you're too innocent to know about them. Next door, wallowing in glamorous squalor, dwells another dreamboat named Claude, an abstract impressionist who claims to be a protégé of Fernand Léger, although I doubt it. Why don't you fly over and join us? Jean-Paul Sartre, Simone de Beauvoir, and Jean Cocteau, *tout le monde*, they're all over the place here. Or so people say. If I hang out at the right *boîte*, I'm told I can run into them. (So far our paths haven't crossed.)

As for my hand-to-mouth existence, I've been hired as a translator for a tiny literary magazine run by some American expats. Not much pay, but I'm navigating a slow boat through the surreal oceans of my most fantastic dreams. You'd probably hate it here.

Living in glorious sin,

Sally

That evening in the overheated living room of their tiny stucco bungalow, Deborah looked up from the lesson plan she was preparing. Seated across from her at the cluttered dining room table was an exhausted Aunt Tziporah, who had just finished washing the dinner dishes. She had hurried home to prepare the evening meal after closing the dress shop at five o'clock. It was her daily ritual for as long as Deborah could remember. On busy Saturdays when farm families came to town for shopping, her aunt would fill a brown paper bag with homemade American cheese sandwiches for lunch, and the two of them, busy with customers, skipped dinner. Those nights, Main Street stores remained open until nine o'clock.

"I heard from Sally today," Deborah said.

Her aunt concentrated on a sweater she was knitting for her niece to wear to work. A person could freeze in that drafty old school building. The sensible wool cardigan would protect Deborah against pneumonia or anything else she might contract from the little ones. "So?" Aunt Tziporah asked. "Did that foolish girl get herself in trouble yet?"

"She's having a wonderful time over there."

"What's so wonderful about rattling around Europe all by herself?"

"She's meeting crazy people."

"There aren't enough crazy people she can meet here? She has to travel thousands of miles?"

"Each country is different, I guess."

"The more they're different, the more they're the same. When I was your age, I was glad to find a job in America. I worked hard in a men's clothing factory and could barely make a living. You American girls have it good in this world and you don't even realize it."

Deborah nodded but said nothing. She should return to her lesson plan, but instead thought about the letter from Paris. Never in a million years, she told herself, would she want to associate with her former roommate's unsavory new friends. Bunch of neurotics. And why would Sally, the member of a military family, choose to live with a man who wasn't clean-shaven? Not to mention those 'Other Things,' which Sally, no virgin, had already learned in college.

Deborah found a carbon copy of the article her friend requested and sent it by boat because airmail would have cost a fortune. She included a letter tinged with passive admiration, something she felt obligated to supply whether she meant it or not.

Dear Sally,

I'm happy that you're leading the Bohemian life at last. Don't worry. I won't report you to my Parent-Teacher Association or, even worse, your beloved Dean Rutherford.

As for me, I'll focus on the adorable little persons in my class at Grammbly Elementary. We are getting ready to celebrate Thanksgiving with fat Pilgrims that the children have drawn with their broken Crayola crayons. (Sometimes they chew on them.) We've assembled masses of pumpkins they've cut out from orange construction paper. You would love the boxy shapes, very modern art, the kind I guess you and your colorful French buddies admire. My class is lively but not unmanageable, and they seem to return my affection for them. They are thriving on phonics, sounding out the words in their sweet voices. It's a joy to teach them how to read. They're learning so fast it's hard for me to keep up with them. They speed through one primer after another in no time.

Your interesting letter about your wild escapades reminded me of that awful Curfew Evening when you were locked out of the dorm and the housemother caught you climbing in through a ground-floor window with two other sophomores. I was not a witness to the crime that night, but when you told me about it, you added, "Sin is as sin does." Remember? History repeats itself.

Love, Deborah

2020

Rosa at the front desk called early that morning. "Marie-Elana, she sprain her ankle and don' clean today." The message took its time sinking in. Like other tenants at Topiary Towers, Deborah couldn't immediately grasp what the immigrant employees were saying to them.

When she expressed her regrets, the receptionist added in her singsongy manner, "But don' forget, the lady in charge she say we have much fun after breakfast. We have a big fun parade here."

Deborah shook her head. A fun Covid event? If Sally were there, she would be rolling on the floor in stitches. "But won't the quarantine keep everyone inside?"

Rosa further explained how residents could watch from the windows and wave to their children and grandchildren as they drove by in a grand procession of decorated cars, horns blasting.

Deborah didn't care to participate in this fiasco. She disliked the noise of unreasonably loud automobile horns. And without a family of her own, she didn't foresee any joy in squinting to read homemade signs that said, "We love you, Grandma Bertha!"

Instead, Deborah took an empty elevator to her mailbox in the lobby and hoped to find mail from Sally, whose postcards always arrived weeks after she returned home from distant lands. No, wait, Deborah told herself, that was last year, before the plague. Nobody was foolhardy enough to travel these days. Not even Sally.

The elevator back to her tiny efficiency apartment held a heavy man named Sol. "Come in," he called out to her in a voice muffled by a mask that featured a glittery American flag. "Come in. Don't be afraid. Two people are allowed but no more."

Deborah hesitated, adjusted her face mask, and decided to live dangerously. If she caught the bug, she caught it. The two elderly people stood facing each other at opposite sides of the elevator. Deborah didn't want to speak to him, but in such a cramped space, she felt it necessary. "How're you doing, Sol?" she asked, knowing she would have to repeat herself at least twice before he would respond.

"What?" he asked.

"How're you doing?"

"Doing? I'm doing nothing. You can just call me Chairman of the Bored. That's spelled b-o-r-e-d."

Deborah tried to smile politely. "What floor do you want?"

"What floors have you got?"

She pressed the button for her floor and the door closed. "Where are you headed?" Sol asked.

"Six," she said, and then another time, slightly louder: "SIX!!"

"That's as good as any." It was like an old-fashioned comic radio routine they shared day after day. When they reached their destination, they carefully stepped out of the elevator and shuffled down the hall together.

"To tell you the truth," Sol said, "I'm not in such good shape. I'm at the doctor's, and she asks me, Mr. Kotsen, how are your bowels, and I say, 'Irritable. Very hard to get along with.' And she didn't even think that was funny." He noticed the lack of expression on Deborah's face. "Don't you think it's a good one?"

Deborah removed a key from her handbag. "Have a nice day," she said. She opened her door and then, not wanting to disturb her neighbors, quietly shut Mr. Kotsen out of her life. Although she believed in being civil, she rarely connected with the other elderly people on her floor. She had nothing to say to them but was willing to answer sensible questions. She recalled a woman last week in the Trash Room. While dumping newspapers into a plastic receptacle, the woman described her fondness for reading obituaries and then turned her interest to the land of the living.

"I heard you were a schoolteacher," she said to Deborah.

"Yes."

"Can you answer this question for me? These days when someone dies, people say 'passed' as if it's too much trouble to add 'away.' Is the expression 'passed away' going out of style?"

"As educators," Deborah said in a serious voice, "we used the verb 'passed' to mark the progress of students at the end of the school year. Either they passed and made it to the next grade or they didn't."

"Thank you," the woman answered, and they rarely exchanged words again.

In the apartment Deborah gathered her own daily newspapers for recycling and plucked from the floor a pair of white cotton socks that had fallen off the bed. Bending over was still no great chore for her. Every morning she spent twenty minutes on a treadmill in the downstairs gym. She had read somewhere that daily exercise delayed aging, but for octogenarians like her it was mostly self-delusion. When she was younger, if she experienced a pain or an itch, she convinced herself that it would disappear in a week or two. But now at this age, nothing ever seemed to go away for good. It always came back.

Exhausted, she lay half-dreaming on the maroon recliner that had once belonged to her aunt. Afternoon nap time was hours away; there was nothing more pressing to do than to think about Sally. How had they grown old without any fanfare? What ever happened to the past? How did they ever manage to stay alive long enough to reach the twenty-first century?

To soothe her nerves, she thought about rereading selected letters written by Sally years ago. But Deborah was in no mood. A relentlessly throbbing ache in her jaw reminded her that she shouldn't put off a necessary visit to the dentist, quarantine or no quarantine. Earlier in the day when she bit into a throat lozenge, a sliver of tooth broke off from her lower right molar. Deborah knew she had to find a fast way to reach the dentist's office. She didn't look forward to ordering a germ-laden taxi in times like these, but she also didn't trust herself to drive anywhere in such pain.

The lockdown had brought strict new rules to Topiary Towers. "If you are going out among people, remember to get your temperature taken in the lobby," Ms. Patel announced. "Then sign out, giving your destination and reason for leaving the building. And get a form from the doctor or dentist confirming the procedure he performed and an evaluation of your condition."

Like college days, Deborah thought. Sally always resented signing out whenever she left the campus evenings and weekends. "Not fair," she said. "The guys never have to do this."

Hours later, sporting a gleaming new crown in her mouth, Deborah headed for home. The pressure on her tooth and the soreness of the gum kept her awake that night. When she turned over in bed, a cramp seared through the flesh in her right thigh, and there was nothing to do but get up and search for a heating pad. By then she was wide awake.

When the pain subsided, she removed from her closet shelf a black mahogany box filled with vintage mail from Sally and a battered Whitman's Sampler box holding carbon copies of Deborah's own letters to her friend. The precious correspondence was worth a visit before Deborah could fall asleep.

1962

Hey Deb,

Please be advised that like General MacArthur, I have returned, albeit jilted and without a sou to my name. So much for Paris in the springtime. Am existing in New York now and will send you a street address when I settle my *tuchus*, which someone told me is Yiddish for fanny.

You're not going to believe this, but I have charmed my way into a job as a junior reporter/researcher for American News & Global Chronicle! How did this happen, you may ask. (Probably not.) My Uncle Tim, a government lawyer with the Department of Commerce, knew somebody who knew somebody. It never hurts. I have the feeling that I'm going to zoom to the top. Soon I'll be getting paid for traveling around the world on assignments, the dream of a lifetime. My boss says he may send me to Cairo one of these days. Meanwhile, my shattered heart is mending. One of my former French lovers used to say, "Absinthe makes the heart grow fonder." Scotch is better. Later will send more details to you, my intrepid Pied Piper of Boxton.

Cheers, Sally

Dear Sally,

Bravo on your success! I'm pressed for time right now because my aunt has just returned from the hospital after a bad fall and needs a lot of attention from me. And also there is a man named Steve who has entered the picture, although I'm reluctant even to mention it because, frankly, I don't think he's worth mentioning.

Love, Deborah

1963

"Steve has a nice word for everybody, hasn't he? He's a good salesman," Aunt Tziporah said after she and her niece finished with the Sunday supper dishes on a spring evening. The dress shop was closed. As usual, Deborah had clerked in the store all day Saturday after a week of standing on her feet next to the blackboard at Grammbly Elementary School. Aunt Tziporah's heavy dinners of stuffed cabbage and boiled potatoes always left Deborah feeling lethargic and defeated. She had put on ten pounds since college and the extra weight was causing lower back strain. All she wanted was to finish clearing away the dishes and loading the small portable dishwasher attached by hose to the kitchen sink. Then she should grade arithmetic papers, but the thought didn't appeal to her.

"Did you hear me?" Aunt Tziporah asked. "Don't you think Steve would be a real catch for some lucky girl?"

Deborah sighed. Throughout her childhood and adolescent years, she had hung onto her aunt's every word, trusting her to be a guardian of truth and Old World wisdom. Early on, Deborah learned the easiest way to get along with her aunt was never to disagree, but this topic of conversation was testing her patience more than she wanted to admit.

"If you like that type," she said.

Deborah felt there was something coarse about her aunt's new employee and his bothersome way of pronouncing the letter "R," not hard, but rather carelessly mush-mouthed. "His voice irritates me," she said. "He's too raspy."

Her aunt persisted. "Get practical, honey. Steve handles the customers better than I do. It was a lucky day when he came to town. The minute I saw him I thought, this young man is something." When Deborah didn't respond, her aunt demanded a better answer. "Don't you think he's really something?"

"I'm glad you hired him, but that doesn't mean I have to date him."

"My customers are crazy about him. He's good-looking, a nice Jewish boy from the city. Has no family. Says he was an orphan like you. You have a lot in common. What more could a girl want in a man?"

Deborah's left foot hurt. She needed to buy a pair of those comfortable Red Cross oxfords to wear on the job. She felt a bunion coming on. "He's just not my type," she heard herself say as she flexed her toes in her pink bunny slippers. Not my type. Sally would have roared at that. Deborah hadn't heard from her friend in ages.

Aunt Tziporah rested her plump hand on Deborah's arm. "Do me a personal favor. Go with him the next time he asks you. A movie. A ride in the country. What harm can it do? You don't have nobody to go out with in this town. My heart breaks for you."

"Maybe it's indigestion," Deborah said, hoping her aunt would change the subject or better still, just stop talking. After all, it was Sunday, Deborah's only day off, and she should make a lesson plan for the week ahead and then relax.

"Even if some yokel from around here would ask, you wouldn't go, would you, my sweet little girl? No. Of course you wouldn't. You and me, we both want some day a nice Jewish wedding with a rabbi and a catered reception for all my relatives in the city, don't we? I wouldn't mind seeing Steve as the groom breaking the glass. He makes a nice appearance, don't you think?"

Deborah didn't want to be bothered. "Give it a rest. Okay? If Steve ever asks me again, which I doubt, I'll go have a cup of coffee with him, but that's all. Just stop jumping on me for once."

"Don't say I'm jumping on you." Tziporah looked crushed. "That's not nice. A dog jumps on you. I'm not a dog. I'm your aunt and I love you. I sent you to college and I always want you to be happy. Is that such a crime?"

"No," Deborah said wearily, "it's not a crime." The crime was she never had the heart to argue with Aunt Tziporah. Or the stamina.

She threw a gray cardigan over her shoulders and headed for the door.

"Where are you going?"

"I need some fresh air for a change."

"I can come with you if you don't go too far."

Deborah pretended she didn't hear and kept walking. Her feet led her down Main Street past the darkened display window of the tiny dress shop. Her youthful immigrant parents had started the business as a family clothing store until their untimely deaths. They left behind an American-born child. Never married, Tziporah felt it was her duty to keep her brother's infant daughter from entering an orphanage. "God forbid you should be raised by strangers," she told Deborah. Often. "Besides, I already lost my job in the men's overcoat factory and didn't have no place else to go. So I left the city for good and moved to the country. I was strong, strong like iron."

Despite the hardships of the Depression, Tziporah managed to transform the abandoned store into a specialty shop selling women's apparel. By also working evenings and Sundays as a dressmaker and tailor, she and the little girl survived. Each year Deborah watched as her aunt lit the memorial yahrzeit candles. "That's so you mustn't forget your mother and father," she said. Deborah learned to recognize their faces only from images pasted in a dreary photo album. She tried to appreciate the blessings about which she was constantly reminded. But it took massive amounts of tolerance to live with someone strong like iron.

Deborah continued her walk as far as Heritage Road where neat hedges of boxwood separated respectable Victorian houses. She relaxed, enjoying the green stability, the righteousness of leafy boundaries. Privacy flourished on this street. Decorum. She liked that.

It was a warm May evening; the daylight stubbornly refused to leave. She could hear her own footsteps on the brick sidewalk with its old-fashioned herringbone pattern. The sound played out a little song she taught her classes. It was based on the Vachel Lindsay poem about a turtle who lived in a box. Her stride kept perfect time to the words she sang in her head. The turtle snapped at a mosquito and then a flea, and finally, according to the childish verse, "It snapped at me." She felt sad to have hurt Aunt Tziporah. I've never been good at snapping at anyone, Deborah thought, not like Sally, who enjoyed raw combat.

When the Milky Way brightened the Boxton sky, Deborah returned home, jotted down the vaguest of lesson plans, kissed her aunt goodnight to show there were no hard feelings, and went to bed. She owed Sally a letter, although in the vast scheme of things, Sally owed Deborah three letters.

1964

Dear Sally,

Big changes here on the home front. My poor aunt has been having kidney trouble. At least she had the good sense to hire Steve Danzig as her right-hand man because I am NOT giving up teaching. If needed, I'll help in the store on Saturdays, but that's it. Steve takes a load off my shoulders.

It seems your career is going full speed ahead. I read an interesting article you wrote about President Kennedy's assassination last November for one of the news magazines, but I don't remember which one it was. It amazes me that you're always on the go, covering important people and places. And thanks for the postcard from Rome. I'm glad you saw the Pope at the Vatican even from a distance. I guess Catholics enjoy that sort of thing. (Joke.) On your trip down the Nile, did you run into King Tut? (Another bad joke.) Let me know what you're up to lately.

Love, Deborah

Before she mailed the letter, Deborah eliminated the references to Catholics and King Tut. The latter could get Sally in trouble, possibly cause an international incident if intercepted by the wrong people. And the former might offend her on religious principles, which varied from one day to the next. One never knew what might rub Sally the wrong way.

1965

Hi Deb,

Yes, I know, you haven't heard from me in ages . . . if not longer. I'll try to break it to you gently. Remember Bill Hadley, our Big Cheese editor-in-chief at State U.? I ran into him in Bordeaux while on assignment in the wine country. (Nice work if you can get it.) Now a freelancer, Bill was headed for Egypt to cover the political situation there.

Anyway, this and that happened. Excessive wine-tasting must have gone to my head because I married the man. Please don't faint. He later insisted I leave my job. It seemed like a good idea because I was quite pregnant at the time. Except for an undying allegiance to Dorothy Day, I've never been anything close to devout, but I did draw the line at an abortion, Bill's ghastly suggestion. Now I'm stuck in a couple of stinky rooms in Queens with a toddler and (gasp) another baby on the way. Talk about *The Long Loneliness*! (Have you ever read that great book by Dorothy? If not, do so right this minute.) How's it going in your little outhouse on the prairie or whatever it is?

Cheers, Sally

Dear Sally,

How wonderful to learn about your marriage and growing family! Congratulations! Or as my aunt taught me to say in Yiddish, Mazel Tov! A few new things have happened here too. My aunt still runs the business with the help of Steve Danzig. Have I mentioned him before? He's a lively person, a little on the earthy side, about ten years older than I am, who used to come to my aunt's shop peddling seasonal women's fashions for a wholesaler in the city. Aunt T. was so impressed with him that she hired him. At first I didn't like Steve much because he was sort of brash (still is) and not terribly interested in things like my Book Club or the Boxton Historical Society, but at least he showed interest in me.

Unlike your storybook romance with Bill, our love seemed to be the kind that nudged itself along. We were married at a rabbi's study in the city. I told my aunt I didn't want to waste money on any unnecessary and expensive fuss. Because she hasn't been well lately, she agreed. Our witnesses were my aunt and the rabbi's wife Hannah. The two of them both came to America from the same village in Poland. I've made Aunt Tziporah very happy. She dotes on her new nephew-in-law. Best news of all, Steve doesn't insist that I quit work and become a full-time housewife.

My principal informed me that next year I'll be handling a combined class of first and second graders. Not easy, but I'll manage. I love everything about my work, even the routine of taking attendance each morning and keeping the children's grades recorded in a little red book also containing my lists of those who order plain milk for recess, those who want chocolate milk at lunchtime, and those who too frequently ask to be excused to go to the bathroom. Last week one little girl didn't quite make it in time. Guess who had to clean her up. Thankfully, that doesn't happen every day.

You might say that Steve and I have a reasonably happy marriage except that on our first wedding anniversary, I had a miscarriage which led to a stay in the hospital and a few complications ending in a hysterectomy. Really no big deal at all. It happens more often than we hear. Nobody talks about it. So while reading about your lovely little child and the coming baby, I was especially happy for you. Please enjoy every minute of it. Some of us are not that lucky. Write when you can.

Love, Deborah

Deborah managed to compose the letter on her new electric typewriter, which she despised but needed for class progress reports to the new principal. Afterward, she retyped it, omitting the entire paragraph about her miscarriage. There was no point in blabbing her troubles to Sally, who couldn't be bothered with ugly sob stories like that.

1967

Dear Deborah,

Yeah, yeah, I know, too much time has gone by without a letter from me. The passing months have brought a sea-change in our lives. Although Bill didn't have a bona fide nervous collapse, he came close. In fact, this past year he abandoned his recent job at the *New York Daily News* for a whole new line of work. We moved. He has become an oyster seed farmer on the Chesapeake Bay. Imagine that! We grow the seeds and sell them to others who turn them into full-grown oysters. As a Navy kid, I can't seem to get away from the water, can I? He and our two kids keep me hopping. Little Sean is a quiet child, but his sister Meghan is turning into one holy terror.

Bill Hadley is not your typical waterman. If you remember in college, he wasn't a typical anything. He took over this oyster business from his cousin but remains a dyed-in-the-wool intellectual devoted to Joyce, Hemingway, and a bit too much Johnnie Walker.

It's beautiful here on the water, lots of unpolluted air and friendly folks, a quieter life, free from the pressures of Gotham. We have an entire little island all to ourselves. Bill thrives in this environment. At least I think he does. I know he'd be glad to see you again. Why don't you come visit for a few days when school lets out?

Your fair-weather friend, Sally

Dear Sally,

It sounds like a marvelous change for you. Boxton is changing fast, too, these days, more new people moving here to work at the meat packing plant and McDonald's is replacing the local Greek family restaurant. Meanwhile, I keep busy turning out little pupils who can read by the end of the school year. Thanks to remarkably good health, I've maintained a perfect attendance record this year. Students who attend school every day receive a Perfect Attendance prize at the annual Awards Assembly in June, but we teachers remain unsung and under-paid. Oh well, that's how it goes.

You'll be glad to learn that Grammbly Elementary School is now finally integrated. It has taken years of community ugliness to reach this point. In Boxton some parents even broke away to organize a private academy. Although they recruited a couple of our best teachers, they tried to sign me up, but I don't agree with their ideas. Remember in college how you and I championed Freedom to Be Educated? That has stuck with me.

One pleasant thing about life as Mrs. Steve Danzig. Although he and Aunt T. have differences of opinion (often loud and emotional), he frees me from a lot of business paperwork, bookkeeping, ordering stock, doing taxes, etc. Steve says he has no desire for me to stay home. All he needs, he says, is a subscription to *Sports Illustrated* and a weekly poker night out with his buddies in the Boxton Volunteer Fire Department. The mother of one of my students said to me the other day, "You and your husband are a model couple in this town. You're such a good influence on our children." I certainly hope so.

It has been a while since hearing from you. What with all that's happening these days, the war and all the crazy drugged hippies running wild, I suspect you have been tempted to resume your journalistic career and get it all down on paper. Right? Please drop me a note when you can.

Love, Deborah

1968

Hi Deb,

Excuse the long, long silence. Bill is writing a book on the hidden glories of oyster growing. He calls me his muse. That's a literary way of saying he expects me to type his manuscript and edit ever-so-sparingly while I'm in the middle of changing diapers on a not-yet-toilet-trained toddler and battling his sister, fiendish little Meghan, who just knocked over and broke my favorite lamp in the living room. I feel like a squeezed orange and have no juice left over.

Can you do me a tremendous favor? I have a pushy friend, Harriet Simpkins. Under a ridiculous nom de plume, she yearns to sell freelance pieces to women's magazines and keeps handing me over-written domestic bilge to critique when I haven't time to wipe my nose. You've always been more of a homebody than I am. You even read *Ladies' Home Journal* back in college. See enclosed. What dost thou think? The truth please. Thanks.

Cheers, Sally

A Young Mother's Tragic Tale
by Fleur Fontaine

Six hundred miles in a car with a toddler and a colicky baby taught me one thing. We mothers swallow any blasted nonsense we read. A housewifely magazine article had assured me that travel with small children could be a breeze. Preparation was the key. The day before departure I stocked up on canned fruit, juices, candy, crackers, cookies, sugar-laden cereals, and fresh fruit. We weren't going to be caught short and ruin a delightful trip. Not us.

While my husband attended all-day business meetings and cocktail parties, the rest of our little family would be sequestered in a nearby mountain resort, where meals were served three times a day. At home our children require five daily meals which they don't eat. They would find it impossible not eating just three in a new location. That's why I kept in my pocketbook tiny cans of tuna and a can opener available at any time of the day or night. Even so, we looked forward to a glorious journey because, as the magazine article maintained, "You'll be surprised how much young children sleep on long motor trips."

Really? It's said that an army travels on its stomach. Ours traveled on mine. Forty miles out, we discovered the older child's security blanket had disappeared. On the spot I weaned her to a moth-eaten, woolen replacement, which I kept handy for catastrophes of this nature. She remained surly but finally draped herself in this substitute coverlet despite the mid-June heat (no air-conditioning in the car). My husband did all the driving. Even though I have no license, I would have been deliriously happy to take over the wheel.

The man I married remained helpless throughout the long haul. During our first hour on the road, he ate all the "emergency only" candy stashed away on the empty passenger seat next to him. He found it impossible to remember that the "Old Faithful" toys and books were piled on top of a dirty clothes hamper near the wash rag and soap bag, which sat next to the garbage receptacle on top of the cooler chest in the back seat. That's where I was doomed to sit. I needed to keep everything at my fingertips because the car trunk was jammed with stroller, playpen, guard rail, three suitcases, and tons of cloth diapers.

Following the magazine advice, we planned to picnic gaily along the way. A recent downpour had left roadside tables puddly and buggy. We ate inside the car, and that was no picnic. We learned, too, there's nothing more wearying than an *endless jaunt with little ones who don't feel secure unless they're clutching a cracker. Not eating, just clutching. At each stop, I shoveled off the front and rear seats. Well before reaching the destination, our offspring were screaming bloodily. For Daddy.*

The trick is to plan ahead? A lie. The real trick is not going at all. Our return trip was not one whit better except that on the second day of travel, fifteen minutes from home, both worn-out kids slumbered blissfully. You'd be surprised how much small children sleep on long motor trips.

Turning the pages, Deborah realized no Harriet Simpkins existed, no Fleur Fontaine. It was all pure Sally. But why would a professional journalist ask for writing advice from a schoolteacher who spent her days on primers filled with "See Jane run"? Was Sally unhappy with her life as a wife and mother? Did she need to put it in writing? And wasn't it somewhat cruel of her to send this article to a dear friend with no babies of her own? Sally remained Sally. Deborah knew that she must continue to play the role her friend had always assigned to her.

> Dear Sally,
>
> Such a wonderful sense of humor your friend has! Any reputable women's magazine will love Harriet's clever approach to sharing travel advice with young mothers. Please tell Harriet that she is a gifted writer and should keep at it.
>
> Love, Deborah

Sally responded months later by sending an envelope packed with standard rejection slips from *Good Housekeeping* and *Woman's Home Companion*, and an index card bearing a desolate message: "Please come visit soon. Am a bit tempest tossed."

1969

"I really hate traveling," Deborah said to Steve after she finished washing dishes left over from her pallid cauliflower-and-tuna casserole. Aunt Tziporah, the official cook of the family, had been warned by the doctor to keep off her feet for a few days. She slumped half-asleep on a plump, goose-gray parlor chair, a recent addition to the shabby cottage where the three of them lived together in dubious harmony.

"I can't put off my trip to Sally's any longer," Deborah continued, "but it disrupts my whole routine, and it's farther away than I want to drive by myself. So I'll have to take two buses and a cab to get there and back."

Aunt Tziporah opened her eyes. "School's out. You could use a few days' vacation."

But Deborah said she had many things to clear up that summer before she began a teachers' workshop at State U. "Steve, do you think I should visit Sally just for a weekend?"

He frowned, concentrating on the ringside arrival of a man he had bet would be the next world's heavyweight boxing champion. "Do what you want," Steve said, not taking his eyes off the TV screen.

"I always feel uncomfortable spending the night anywhere other than in my own bedroom," Deborah said.

Aunt Tziporah opened her eyes. "Don't make such a big *tzimmes* out of everything, Deborah. Go and enjoy yourself for a change. Am I right, Steve?"

Steve muttered something that neither woman could hear.

"Maybe I should," Deborah said to Steve. "It's a chance for a nice visit with Sally and her little family. We haven't seen each other since college." She turned to her aunt. "Do you really think I ought to go?"

"Didn't you once tell me she married a *shikkōr*?" Aunt Tziporah asked. "A crazy drunkard?"

"I'm sure Bill gave up his bad habits long ago. I mean, people grow older and live and learn." Deborah glanced at her overweight husband and added under her breath, "Some do anyway."

"I'd go with you, but it's too much for me right now," Aunt Tziporah said. "Maybe better you should stay home. I'll worry too much about you."

"Except," Deborah said, "I can't refuse Sally."

"You and your Sally. If she ever told you to jump off the roof, would you do it?"

Deborah gave her aunt a tolerant smile. "Depends on how far away the ground is," she said.

During her first evening at the shabby beach house on the Chesapeake, Deborah noted something odd. At college Sally had often chugalugged cheap whiskey with assorted boyfriends. Now she served no alcohol, nothing before, during, or after dinner, not even the local beer. They must be struggling to make ends meet in this unpredictable oyster-growing business, Deborah thought. Bill Hadley glumly sipped iced tea along with the stone-cold Kentucky fried chicken he had picked up on his way home from the dock. The two small children competed for attention throughout dinner and shrieked in unison when their mother tried to bed them down.

Drowning in chaos, Sally found little time to talk with her guest. Deborah was left alone to share long silences with Bill, whom she had never liked. She went to bed early, and after spending the night on a lumpy rollaway cot with no pillow, Deborah came down to the breakfast table. A stack of lukewarm pancakes awaited her.

"I made these from scratch!" Sally said proudly. "The secret is adding sour cream."

Deborah took a first bite. "They're delicious," she said, because that was what Sally wanted to hear.

"These are the worst flapjacks you've ever made." Bill threw down his fork and made a rude gagging sound in his throat. "They make me puke!" He glared at her. Sally appeared crushed to be pilloried in front of an old friend.

"Oh, I think they're quite good," Deborah said with more ordinary enthusiasm than needed. Sally gave her a weary but grateful smile.

Bill fixed his eyes on Deborah and snarled, "Shut your face. I wasn't talking to you." He deliberately knocked his plate to the floor and stalked out.

Sally ran after him. "You come back here!" she screamed. "You come back here and apologize, you arrogant shit-faced son of a bitch!" Then she rushed to the breakfast table where Deborah sat stunned, not knowing how to react. The two women stared at each other until Sally gave a nervous little laugh.

"Excuse my French," she said with an artificial grin on her face. "Bill's nose is out of joint because they rejected the final draft of his book yesterday. Don't mind him. I'm sure he loves having you here. I know I do." She leaned over to hug Deborah, who remained silent. "I'm so sorry, Deb."

"It's all right," Deborah said, breaking away. "Let me help you clean up this mess."

"No, just sit. You're my guest."

Sally grabbed a broom and plastic dust pan to clear the food from the kitchen floor. Deborah stayed quiet, expecting Sally to offer more details about the darkness of living with an alcoholic husband. Her friend chose that moment to answer the cries of Sean in the playpen, and meanwhile, belligerent Meghan, who had been digging in her sandbox outside, entered with a significant load in her pants.

"Double trouble," Sally said, rocking Sean in her arms. "Excuse the smell. Neither of these two little demons is toilet-trained yet. I spend my entire day changing diapers."

Deborah decided to cut her visit short by pretending to come down with a nasty sore throat. "I would never forgive myself if I infected your little ones," she said in her most apologetic voice.

Two years after her depressing visit to the Chesapeake Bay cottage, Deborah received a postcard, totally black, with the caption "Prince Edward Island at Night." Scribbled on the back in the blank space next to the Boxton address was a note in Sally's nearly illegible handwriting:

> Hey Deb, I divorced Bill. Dropped Meghan and Sean off to live with paternal grandparents, who'll adopt the kids. Am free as the great outdoors, vacationing now with blond Adonis named Bob McDuff, nothing serious. Will send new Manhattan address later. If you ever decide to break your marital shackles, you can always move in with me. Ever consider a threesome? Forever available, Sally

Although the divorce didn't surprise Deborah, she resented the casual evaluation of her own marriage. Did Sally imply that the relationship with Steve was too flimsy to last? Or had she meant to be hurtful? Although rarely unkind on purpose, she would never earn a gold star for sensitivity. Probably she wanted to lighten the situation in her own sophisticated way. Deborah's sincere response was brief:

> Hi, Sally, I'm sorry to learn the bad news. Thanks for the thoughtful invitation to join you, but no thanks. One man in one lifetime is more than enough for me.

But when Deborah wrote this, she did not expect the domestic mayhem that lay directly ahead of her.

1970

Aunt Tziporah had no qualms about speaking her mind. Surrounded by racks of cheap housedresses and old-fashioned wooden counters piled high with roughly woven wool sweaters and imitation leather handbags, a tacky confrontation played out one Saturday night after she closed her dress shop.

"Don't lie to me, Steve," Aunt Tziporah said, her face red with anger. "I saw you with my own eyes. You made five sales and you never rang anything up on the cash register. You thought I wasn't looking, but I saw you take the money and put it in your pants pocket."

"You're dreaming again, Tziporah. I did no such thing." He turned to Deborah, who was straightening a table covered with polyester blouses left behind in a heap by the evening's customers. "Tell your old-maid aunt she's over the hill and it's time for her to retire altogether." Deborah looked away for a moment and then quietly continued reorganizing the merchandise.

His answer did not satisfy Aunt Tziporah. "It's not the first time. I've seen you do it before. Deborah, did you know about this *gonif*, this thief?"

Deborah wanted it to be over. Most of all, she wanted to be home, grading papers or planning for February. Her class would make valentines from red construction paper. They would vote to pick the lucky student who would serve as mail carrier. Everyone would be excited to drop their valentines into the pretty red and white box she had decorated for them.

"Deborah, for God's sake don't stand there like a dummy on display in the window. This time I caught him red-handed. At least say something."

Her niece continued to sort out the blouses size by size. She felt frozen into this shoddy scene. It was a Main Street tableau that Norman Rockwell would never have submitted as a *Saturday Evening Post* cover.

Steve grabbed the pile of clothing Deborah had just put in order and, with one gesture, knocked everything to the beige carpeting. "Will you stop for just a minute?" he said. "If you don't tell the old bat once and for all to shut her trap, I'll shut it for her."

Deborah knelt to gather up the merchandise scattered on the floor. She didn't look at Steve, who continued to yell. "You want the truth, Tziporah? Okay, here it is in spades. I owe lots of money to certain people right now, okay? And I couldn't wait for you to dole it out to me like I was some charity case."

"I always give you both everything you need," Tziporah said. "All you have to do is ask."

He lowered his voice and spoke directly to Deborah. "There's a big race at Pimlico coming up next week. I had a hot tip this afternoon, a long shot. Terrific odds. I'll be able to pay back everybody I been borrowing from. Including you."

"A gambler is a gambler," Tziporah announced solemnly in a moment of conveying what she considered to be wisdom of the ages. "You can bake him, cook him sweet and sour, but he stays a gambler."

Steve turned again to Deborah, who was once more carefully sorting the blouses according to size. "Honey, I swear on my mother's grave, I'll make it good," he said. "Trust me, you'll get back every cent. Plus interest."

Deborah took her time placing the merchandise on a nearby shelf.

"What do you say?" Steve demanded. "Pay attention for a change."

Time for her to speak up. In the same spot, what would Sally do? Deborah knew. "It's more than nickels and dimes," she said with a firmness that surprised even herself. "I've known for years about your creative bookkeeping."

"What are you talking about?"

"The two sets of books."

"He keeps two sets of books?" Tziporah said, outraged. "I knew something wasn't right. What was I thinking to let a nix, a nothing like him, handle the bookkeeping?"

Steve dismissed the charge with an indifferent wave of his hand. "You have no proof. Where's your proof?"

Deborah sighed. It all had to rise to the surface now. "I found them in an old file drawer somebody forgot to lock," she said. She had known for a long time, always waiting for a more comfortable moment to confront him. Postponing came easy; but now this final unpleasantness had forced her to speak up. Even so, she preferred not to mention his womanizing on his out-of-town buying trips. She had known about that for years too.

Steve addressed his remarks solely to her. "Honey, you always had a kind heart. Right here and now, I promise you to give it all up. I'm taking no more chances. I won't even look at a punchboard at the candy store. For old time's sake, can't you forgive and forget, after all we've been through together?" He tried to take her hand, but she pulled it away.

"Forgive and forget?" Tziporah yelled, taking up a well-worn refrain. "You talk about forget? A man who misses his first wedding anniversary and leaves his sick little wife to suffer alone at home?"

No, Deborah thought, not that again. This wasn't the time or place. Not now, not here.

"That's enough," she said in a dead voice.

Steve's face reddened as he answered the accusations. "How would I know what was going on with her? She didn't say nothing except she had a pain in her stomach. She told me it wasn't so bad. It would go away."

"A miscarriage doesn't go away," Aunt Tziporah said. "You're the one who went away. You didn't care what happened to her."

"I cared plenty." He turned to Deborah. "Didn't I send you a big bouquet of red roses? Cost me a fortune. And when I came home from my buying trip, I even brought you a nice magazine to cheer you up at the hospital, remember?"

Deborah closed her eyes. "I don't want to hear this," she said.

Her aunt defended herself as she usually did during these endless clashes. "I didn't know where or how to reach you. And when the doctor ordered a hysterectomy right away and warned me I could lose her altogether, what was I supposed to do?"

"It was my decision," Deborah said in a monotone. "Not yours."

Tziporah's voice softened. "No, I let you do it. I was too hasty. I'll never forgive myself." Tears ran down her flushed face. Deborah put an arm around her aunt's shoulders and wondered what Sally would do. Underplay the situation? Or make an irrelevant joke to lighten the moment? What could be a reasonable response?

She found herself speaking with an air of quiet authority, a voice she used when disentangling a fight over a game of marbles in the schoolyard. "Why bring all this up again? It's been years. It happened a long time ago, and it's over."

"It's not over," Aunt Tziporah said. "I think about it every day. You have no babies. You never will." Deborah turned away and slowly walked to the plate-glass door at the entrance to the shop. She looked outside. The street was empty; at least no late Saturday-night shoppers remained outside to overhear this tacky episode and report it to their neighbors the next morning at church.

"You and I can work it out," Steve said as he followed her. He moved closer and tried to grab her arm, but she pulled away and continued to walk. If Sally were there, she would have shouted, "YAY Deb!"

"No," she said in a sharp tone she had never used with Steve. "We trusted you, and you deceived us." Most likely, Sally would have chosen more colorful words, but that kind of coarseness was the sin for which teachers punished nasty children who scribbled such language on the faded bricks of Grammbly Elementary. She wasn't going to sink to that level. "You've lied to me for years," she said in a deadly quiet voice.

He gave a false laugh. "We're married, kid. I'm entitled to lie."

Aunt Tziporah had caught her breath and returned to the battlefield. "You're entitled to nothing, that's what you're entitled to. The store is mine and after I go, it belongs to Deborah."

He gave her a cynical smile. "So what are you going to do? Throw me in the county jail?"

At the cash register on a counter near the store entrance, Deborah carefully counted out ten twenty-dollar bills and turned to him. "Take this, buy yourself a bus ticket, and leave. I never want to see you in here again." The words came out of her with little effort, as if she were calmly reprimanding one of her pupils for secretly chewing gum in class.

He didn't surprise her when he took the money. As he counted it, he shook his head. "This is your best offer? Two hundred lousy bucks for putting up with both of you all these years?"

A fake audience laugh track would come in handy now, Deborah thought. Both Steve and her aunt were like faded comedians in a third-rate TV show, a flop that wouldn't be returning the next season.

Deborah gave him what she considered a chilling look. "If you ever come back to Boxton, if you ever dare to set one foot in this town again, I'll see that you spend most of your days in the state prison for embezzlement."

He thrust the money into his pocket, stared deeply into her eyes, and delivered his final shot. "You know," he said in the raspy voice that Deborah thought captured his pervasive vulgarity, "you have a face only a mother could love." And then he was gone. Off to the races, Deborah thought.

1971

All for the best, Deborah told herself. She would clean up the financial mess, but one thing was certain. There must be no damage to her reputation in the community. She wanted her students to remember their teacher fondly, not as the wife of a thief. Her answer to anyone who inquired about Steve's disappearance would be simple and low-key. "I guess he just didn't like living in a small town," she said. A year later she quietly obtained an uncontested divorce on the grounds of desertion.

Although Deborah didn't miss Steve, Aunt Tziporah felt the impact of his absence. She was forced to hire local housewives to work in the shop on busy Saturdays when farmers and their families flocked to town. As she grew older, she changed her refrain. "Maybe you shouldn't have sent him away," she said.

"Steve was better than nothing. When I go, you'll be all alone. No husband, no kiddies."

"I can do without him," Deborah said.

"Listen to me. Write him. Call him. There's nobody here for you. Tell him you want him back."

"I don't even know where he is."

"It was easier with him than without him."

"He robbed us blind."

"You married him, Deborah. He was a member of our family. What am I going to do? The business is not what it was. Did you notice in the paper? Big chain stores are coming to town. They'll put us out of business altogether."

"Hang on as long as you can," Deborah said a bit too cheerfully.

"I'm not getting any younger and neither are you."

"There's always my salary to fall back on, and later I'll have my teacher's pension." Deborah attempted to add a little humor. "If worse comes to worst, Sally will rescue us."

"When the Messiah comes," Aunt Tziporah said and added, "She knows about you and Steve?"

"Not yet." Deborah could not bring herself to share a personal failure like that. It would diminish her in Sally's eyes.

Ever since college, Deborah considered their alliance fragile, easily shattered. Although Sally was no paragon, the excitement of knowing her, romanticizing her, was too valuable to be abandoned even if they rarely saw each other. Women needed to hold onto threads of their younger days, she told herself. A movie, a song, or an acquaintance like Sally. Anything would do.

"Some friend!" Aunt Tziporah said. "You never hear from her. Maybe you shouldn't bother with her no more."

"Never in a million years," Deborah said, knowing her aunt could interpret those words any way she wished. "Anyway, I think she's somewhere in South America right now. There's too much going on for her to write me letters."

1972

Hi Deb,

Oy vey and gefilte fish! I'm back home now and spending more days in Manhattan than on the road. Not for long. I'm off to Sweden next week to cover the Nobel extravaganza. Here's something to interest you. Most of my neighbors in this apartment house are Jewish, and sometimes I think I know more Yiddish than the lot of them. By the way, a close friend of mine died last week. She was the matriarch of a bitterly embattled family. (That's something we Irish have in common with you folks.) As a favor, her son asked me to host a Shiva at my place! (Yes, things were that bad.) So I did it. Fascinating. I'll tell you more perhaps when I see you next, which, considering my erratic schedule these days, may be in the sweet bye and bye.

Love, Sally

Sally consoling mourners at a Shiva? Deborah knew the routine; she had attended a few traditional funerals with Aunt Tziporah in the city forty miles away. After burial, attendees, mostly elderly immigrants, crowded into the home of the deceased, where mourners sat on small, low chairs. A quorum of ten men assembled for a late afternoon service to recite Kaddish with bereaved family members. Women guests stayed in the kitchen throughout the prayers. At intervals the unlocked front door opened and clusters of people apprehensively entered bearing bakery goods. They spoke gentle words of comfort, chatted briefly with anyone they knew, and didn't stay too long. Bustling heavy-set ladies served a home-cooked meal only to the immediate family.

In Boxton Deborah had been to numerous Christian funerals, mostly out of respect for her aunt's longtime customers. But Shiva wasn't like a wake with alcohol flowing or a chatty celebration of life punctuated by a mournful folksinger with a guitar. Sally's Shiva at her Manhattan place must have been classier, much more cosmopolitan, with recordings of classical violin music played by Jascha Heifetz and dry martinis served by a white maid. Deborah pictured Sally in the thick of it, accessible to all, the Irish eyes smiling, a discreet gold cross dangling from a chain around her neck.

1980

Debilitating arthritis ended Aunt Tziporah's reign at the dress shop. No longer was she spry enough to dress the mannequins in the display window or kneel to pin up hems for customers. Her eyes began to fail her. "I can't even thread a needle or sew on a button in the right place," she said.

At a neighboring furniture store, she selected a maroon-colored reclining chair, which Deborah placed just inside the front entrance of the shop. Here the old woman could greet her loyal customers and flatter them when they stepped out of the tiny dressing booth to view themselves in a floor-length mirror. She had always been a shrewd businesswoman, and now she found more time to snap up several Main Street properties. By the time she died peacefully in her bed, she had succeeded in leaving her niece "well-fixed."

Sally did not attend the funeral. She was out of the country, covering a devastating Turkish earthquake that killed hundreds. Deborah assumed that her journalist friend viewed death as nothing special. What was Aunt Tziporah to her? Deborah waited three months before sending the *Boxton Banner* obituary with a brief notation: "You probably don't remember her, but I thought you might want to know."

Sally surprised her with an immediate handwritten note: "Of course, I remember your Aunt Tziporah. We met at the State U. graduation. She was the sweetest person. I can only imagine how much it hurts to lose her." Deborah interpreted this as the healthy revival of their correspondence, but she didn't care to go into the details of her aunt's passing. To infuse her own letters with actual news that would appeal to her friend, Deborah described a scandalous court case involving Boxton's most prominent lawyer. "In a speedy trial," she wrote, "the jury found this man not guilty of murder after he shot and killed a trespasser on his property. Injustice, huh?"

She didn't wish to go further into it with a boring denunciation of gun proliferation, even though it was one of Sally's favorite topics. She chose to end with a more emotional bit of news: "Another unfortunate thing has happened. I am very sad that our historic Masonic Temple on Main Street has been demolished, to be replaced by a Wells Fargo Bank. My town is slowly disappearing before my eyes."

When it came to their correspondence, certain topics remained off-limits. Deborah often wondered why Sally had abandoned her children for a reckless life of roaming the world. Did she feel regret? Had she ever visited her daughter and son? Did she love them? Over the years she never referred to them in her letters. "None of my business," Deborah told herself.

In those lonely months after Tziporah's funeral, Deborah found it painful to sort through a mass of ordinary odds and ends: tangles of embroidery thread, hooks without eyes and eyes without hooks, tarnished thimbles, coffee cans heavy with orphaned buttons, the legacy of an immigrant seamstress. And underneath it all, an envelope bulging with black-and-white Kodak snapshots of Deborah in her Girl Scout uniform.

"It's so hard to go through my aunt's personal belongings," she confided to Anita Hargrove, the second grade teacher at Grammbly Elementary. "Sometimes I get very sad." Each day they ate their brown-bag lunches in an old storeroom converted to a faculty lounge. Anita had become a close friend among the teaching staff, but she was no Sally.

"When my mom passed away last year," Anita said, "I couldn't believe all she accumulated. Even from the grave, we don't know what to expect from our dearly beloved."

Dearly beloved. Deborah bit into her peanut butter and jelly sandwich and mused over the unfamiliar words. Because she had never known her parents, how could she call them dearly loved? Had she loved Aunt Tziporah? Of course, but not dearly. That was too effusive. Adequately, perhaps. And Steve? What would be the direct opposite of dearly? It all depended on the definition of Love. Early in her unremarkable marriage, Deborah reached a practical conclusion. For her, Love was not a full-blown emotion but a courtesy born of obligation. Accepting that idea for ten years of married life had rendered sex with her husband a little less disgusting.

With her aunt gone, Deborah immediately sold the failing dress shop and treated herself to a Queen Anne in the Historic Preservation District. The house once belonged to a sea captain who had added a copper-trimmed balcony, finished off to look like the deck of a nineteenth-century ship. The jutting mermaid on the masthead suggested a stage set for *H.M.S. Pinafore*. Deborah looked forward to a time when she could show it to Sally, who belonged to a Navy family and probably wouldn't be able to hide her envy.

Two blocks away from her classroom, Deborah lived alone in Victorian splendor, sometimes housing younger teachers who marked time at Grammbly Elementary until they found better positions elsewhere. Her friend Anita took a job in Omaha and moved to Nebraska to be near her ailing father. Although Deborah missed their lunches together, she found solace in small things. She enjoyed walking three blocks to work each day. In winter she would stop to admire smiling snowmen built by children whose names she couldn't always remember. Summertime she would bump into them at the county library and praise them for using their vacation time to good advantage. At the 4-H pool, she'd applaud as she watched a parade of her former pupils jump from the high diving board into the water. At Hallowe'en, costumed trick-or-treaters—past, present, and future students—crowded onto her wrap-around front porch as she smilingly dropped into each shopping bag a single lemon-flavored lozenge. "Too much candy is not good for your teeth," she warned the children.

Forever loyal to the school, she never considered leaving. She enjoyed seeing generations of children grow up before her eyes and took pride in their triumphs. Each June she faithfully attended their high school graduations and applauded heartily when they received their diplomas. She felt obligated. After all, it was she who had taught them to read.

2000

In the years that rattled by, Deborah felt herself growing older. Not a woman who favored artificiality, she avoided coloring her hair and patiently watched as gray strands invaded and conquered. Sally, of course, stayed forever young. "Hey, Deb," she wrote in one of her increasingly rare letters, "they say that seventy is the new fifty. It may not be the case in pokey little Boxton, but here in Gotham during this invigorating year of the Millennium, I see proof positive. Advice from a model I interviewed during Fashion Week: use castor oil on your face to prevent wrinkles. I did this to the bags under my eyes, and now at least I have oily bags."

During the weeks when Sally was writing a series of articles on retirement communities in the New York area, she rewarded Deborah with monthly phone calls laden with tart descriptions of installations at the Museum of Modern Art. Or praise of Paul Taylor dance concerts. Or cynical evaluations of off-Broadway plays about clinically depressed people, as she put it. Deborah looked forward to reading these pieces by an authentic New York insider.

Most of all, she loved Sally's letters laden with tart commentary on well-known people she interviewed or newsworthy events that she eye-witnessed during her worldwide adventures. Although Deborah found it tiring to keep track of Sally's whereabouts, she never let herself forget that her friend's byline was recognized by readers throughout the country. Best of all, Sally hadn't officially severed the tie between them. Not yet anyway.

Dear Deb,

This will be short and sweet . . . or as sweet as I'll ever get. I'm here in The Hague to cover an international convention on climate change, and I dreamed of you last night. You drove me and a handsome young Dutch man to a gigantic dairy where they gave us two small pats of butter to use when and how we liked. Seemed goofy as we were told to separate and chomp where we slept. But we reunited and returned safely to our hotel because you were driving our taxi, and you always know where you're heading. Odd, no? Although we trod our separate paths, and while it's usually soothing to find you in my dreams, please butt out and let me discover what happens next between me and the young Lowlands Lothario!

Love, Sally

2002

Dear Sally,

I had to sell my Queen Anne house (which you never visited!!!) because I could no longer climb stairs to reach the only bathroom. One icy morning, I lost my footing on the front porch steps and had another nasty fall. Clumsy me. The right leg hasn't been the same since. Walking has become difficult even with a cane. I hate to leave the beautiful old homestead, which was built in 1889, but I knew deep-down the time would come. The buyer was our former mayor, one of my former pupils, imagine that. The hardest thing about moving was sifting through the many items accumulated from children I've taught. As you'd imagine, I couldn't resist bringing lots of the dearest odds and ends with me.

I'll say goodbye to Grammbly Elementary in June. Recently I bought an apartment at striking Topiary Towers, a retirement facility nearby. On the front lawn you'll find extraordinary landscaping that includes topiaries of gigantic squirrels and bunnies.

Thinking of you, Deborah

She deleted "Thinking of you" and replaced it with "Hoping you're well." She didn't want to insult Sally, who might infer that her active sex life put her in the same category as prolific rodents. A response came faster than usual.

Hello Deb,

Please recover quickly from your mishaps. You've been in my prayers, such as they are. Right now I'm back in New York and up to my neck in a series on U.S. Catholic charities, which I won't go into because it wouldn't interest you. Quite often it doesn't interest me. I do want to visit you soon. If I could once navigate the Amazon River in search of indigenous tribes, you can trust me to hack my way through your Boxton topiaries to find you.

Truth is, I was badly shaken by the horrible destruction of the World Trade Center last year, so mired in gloom I found myself a new shrink, who has marginally saved me. Let's just say that something called *agape* has a lot to do with my new and strangely comforting peace of mind. Be prepared to meet my inner Mother Teresa. Hope to bless you soon, my Hebraic child.

Cheers, Sally

Agape? Deborah consulted her 1973 *Encyclopedia Britannica.* She had never encountered the word before. After pages about the influence of St. Augustine, she dozed off. Agape came from the Greek, meaning "love." In this case it meant Christian love. She put away the heavy book. It's not likely I'll ever have an occasion to use that word, she thought. In their early days at college, Sally experienced these deep-seated epiphanies every other semester. As always, it would pass.

Between the two women, religion never reared its divisive head, at least not openly. Sally avoided cards bearing Nativity scenes and learned to wish Deborah a Happy New Year via tipsy snowmen guzzling champagne. In turn, Deborah sent lighthearted greetings from puppies wearing Santa hats. Still, Deborah sensed their friendship was languishing. Cryptic notes scribbled at the bottom of birthday cards no longer counted. Random phone calls were too trivial, intermittent emails too perfunctory.

When she turned seventy-two, Deborah's teaching career ended. Her departure was marked by a token retirement party in the school auditorium and a Certificate of Excellence for having lasted longer at Grammbly than any other teacher in its entire history. The *Boxton Banner* ran a farewell article about her, accompanied by an unflattering photo, which she thought made her look like a female Winston Churchill. In her handwritten letters, she never mentioned any of this fuss to Sally. Compared to her friend's glittering achievements, the rewards of a nondescript primary schoolteacher seemed provincially dreary, the tiniest of small potatoes.

The more she dwelled on it, the more Deborah worried that her un-answered letters were too boring. She thought perhaps if she made them more poetic, her efforts would rate a faster response. "Dear Sally," she began in a spurt of creativity, "Somehow I feel that the months since we touched base have dissolved like aspirin cast upon the waters." She stopped and ripped the note to pieces.

After no word from her friend in more than a year, Deborah convinced herself that an old temptation had returned to bedevil Sally. No doubt she had Met Somebody again. Several years earlier she had described a Central Park bench encounter with an elderly Jewish stranger playing Mendelssohn on a flute. "Before parting, we exchanged phone numbers. Yes, I know, Deb, you do not approve, but he could become the love of my life if I have the strength. Truth is, I feel lost without a man in my bed. By the way, full retirement is a no-no for me. I still identify myself on the tax form with the mystical words 'freelance writer.' Forever sexy, S."

The more she thought about it, the more Deborah doubted her friend had ever been sincerely interested in her or the placid life she led in Boxton. On sleepless nights, Deborah questioned the longevity of a friendship that had withered on the vine. Be honest, demanded a voice within, why bother? In the past, Sally answered letters only when she didn't have much else to do, which was seldom. Deborah weighed the pros and cons of their sporadic relationship. Even if Sally should feel obligated to respond, Deborah didn't want that brand of charity.

At her rolltop desk, she carefully penned fateful words. "Dear Sally, perhaps we should stop beating a dead horse. Why don't we just satisfy ourselves with mental telepathy, simply thinking of each other at the same time of day, maybe once a week or at least once a month?"

She could think of nothing more to add. After staring for several moments at her message, Deborah neatly crossed out every word, crumpled the lavender notepaper, and tossed it into her trash basket. Whatever remained of their friendship, it was better than nothing, just as Steve had been better than nothing. She liked to entertain herself by imagining what Sally would have done if the two women had swapped lives. Deborah knew the result. Sally wouldn't have married a man like Steve in the first place. But Bill Hadley was no prize package either. The thought always gave her comfort.

2008

"To paraphrase Ecclesiastes: *Of the making of old people there is no end.*" Back in the 1980s Sally had used that sentence in a magazine piece about future Social Security deficits. Now, twenty-five years later, as a resident of Topiary Towers, Deborah agreed. She could not overlook the elderly human turnover in the apartments around her. Each year, as ailing residents faded away, newly minted ones continued coming. Although she had celebrated more birthdays than most of these aging invaders, she couldn't help but think that they all looked older than she did.

She never pretended to love any of her fellow seniors. Only Sally was worthy of true friendship; only the frayed ties of youth were worth salvaging. Deborah acknowledged that the entire world changed when it succumbed to the Cyber Madness, her own private name for it. She came late to the computer and didn't like it one bit. Browsers, servers, apps, blogs, and the entire concept of instant communication left Deborah tired and cranky. She begrudged every minute of dependence on a system she couldn't fathom or control. Her impatient fingers were forever hitting wrong keys that led her deeper into the electronic jungle of no return. The infernal contraption gobbled up more time and energy than it deserved. Although she tried to adapt, she preferred the satisfaction of penning letters in dignified cursive handwriting. Sensible persons would surely agree with her.

The months and years also brought change to Topiary Towers under new management. The workforce fluctuated from year to year. Executive Directors came and then drifted away. Energetic Activities Managers held sway for brief intervals only to leave for higher ground and better pay. Nurses, doctors, cooks, waitresses, and maintenance people never stayed longer than a year or two. Deborah didn't bother to remember names of employees or residents. Whatever would be, would be.

During one major personnel upheaval, Tammy, a former rabbinical student turned social worker, joined the staff and visited Topiary Towers twice a week. Pleased to find a rare Jewish person in the community, Deborah sought help from the younger woman. Perhaps with her theological background, she might be able to translate at least the title of a strange cheesecloth-wrapped book Aunt Tziporah had left behind.

"This is a real treasure," Tammy said in a surprised voice. "Where did you find it?"

"I inherited it. My guess is that our family brought it over from Poland when they first came to this country. I don't know what to make of it. Do you?"

The young woman carefully turned a yellowed page. "It's a Yiddish version of the Torah and the Prophets, written especially for Jewish women. Versions of it appeared between the fifteenth and eighteenth centuries. As you may know, females were forbidden to study Hebrew." Tammy did not lift her eyes from the text as she spoke. "This book enabled wives and mothers to become familiar with sacred literature in their everyday language."

Deborah pointed to the title. "Can you translate this for me? My aunt could speak and read Yiddish, but I grew up here in Boxton and never had much Jewish education."

"It says *Tze-enah u-Re'enah*. The title means 'Go forth and behold!'" Tammy gently closed the book. "Good advice for everybody everywhere."

"I guess."

Tammy handed it back to Deborah. "Thank you for showing this to me. It's priceless, a real family heirloom to pass from one generation to the other."

"I was an orphan, and I have no family to leave it to," Deborah said, surprising herself by volunteering such personal information to a stranger.

Tammy gave her a sympathetic look. "What happened to your mother and father?"

"They both died in a diphtheria outbreak."

"When was this?"

"I was a baby at the time. Back in the early 1930s, I guess."

"Wasn't there an inoculation against the disease?"

"My Aunt Tziporah said my parents didn't have much trust in doctors. Neither did she."

Tammy consulted the papers on her clipboard and discovered she had an appointment coming up in the next hour. "I have to go," she said. "Take good care of your inheritance. If you ever decide to donate it, I'm still in touch with some of my former colleagues at the Seminary. We'll find an appropriate place for it."

After Tammy left, Deborah stared at the peculiar book in her hands. *Go forth and behold!* Old-fashioned words, she thought, not language someone would use at the supermarket. Even so, if she boiled it down to ordinary English it just added up to *Live and learn.* Deborah felt disappointed. She had hoped these pages would contain deep mystical advice, not Bible stories. The book must have meant something to Aunt Tziporah or else why had she protected it all those years?

She couldn't quite rid herself of uneasy thoughts. She didn't know exactly what this strange Yiddish volume demanded of her. She felt torn. Keep it? Donate to a museum or library? Sell on the Internet? She had read somewhere that well-worn sacred Hebrew bibles and prayer books must be buried rather than destroyed. Were the pages still considered holy if written in a secular language?

Deborah briefly pictured herself mentioning the book to Sally. No, not a good idea. Her friend would surely fire off a lengthy condemnation of male chauvinism rooted in every established religion. Deborah didn't care to be reminded of the Women's Lib thing at this stage of her life. Even when she was younger, she let all that hysteria pass her by. She would return the decaying relic to a shelf in the hall closet until a later time. Out of sight, out of mind.

2012

When a message from Sally did arrive at last, it was skimpy and, to Deborah's horror, keyboarded entirely in lowercase.

> hey deb my significant other chaim levy moved in for a couple
> of months until spring he has problems losing teeth (not i) 2
> weeks ago saw opera aida 1930s style live and cartoons i hope
> u are well love s.

The complete disregard for order upset Deborah. As a lifelong journalist, as a State U. English major, for heaven's sake, Sally knew better. She could be forgiven for succumbing to digital expediency when her job depended on it. But why, Deborah wondered, should a professional writer abandon the disciplines of punctuation, spelling, and clarity when it came to personal correspondence? It amounted to sheer laziness and disrespect for hard-working teachers everywhere.

As in all things, Sally had gone overboard, overtaken by the Cyber Madness. Deborah vowed she would never let it enslave her. She continued to avoid the Internet and when in need of historical or literary information, virtuously turned to her 1973 *Britannica* edition. The laptop continued to rattle her nerves; it did nothing to uplift her or revive the fading connection with Sally.

Instead of an occasional electronic snippet, Deborah preferred those earlier and friendlier airmails from Sally, handwritten and postmarked London, Sydney, Bruxelles. The ribbon-tied bundles of airmail envelopes filled the mahogany box stored in a hall closet. Pushed aside on the floor, next to a dark heap of fur-lined galoshes and boots, stood a lopsided cardboard carton. It bulged with mementos of Deborah's teaching days, the faded notebooks filled with lesson plans, crayon drawings by favorite pupils, gift cologne bottles, and accompanying notes from grateful mothers.

It was at the bottom of the carton that Deborah discovered The Magazine waiting for her. Here's an old friend I haven't seen in years, she thought. As she turned the faded pages that lonely evening, she sensed the companionship of an entire era gone by. She cradled it in her arms with an overwhelming tenderness and carried it into her bedroom. Bits and pieces of dead pages dropped behind her, forming a trail. It was like a Hansel and Gretel path scattered to keep her from getting lost in the past. What a silly idea, Deborah thought. She removed a whisk broom from a dresser drawer, knelt on aching knees, and solemnly swept up the papery flakes.

As the hour grew late, she switched into her pink flannel nightgown and carried The Magazine into bed with her. Careful not to tear the disintegrating pages, she reread innocent short stories about flawed marriages that eventually ended well. She smiled at photos of chubby toddlers shown in articles about potty training and remembered her long-ago trip to visit Sally, Bill, and their children. In one mid-century illustration for a piece of short fiction, the heroine wore her auburn hair pulled back, forming a bun at the nape of her neck, a hairstyle favored by that incorrigible redhead back in college days. Deborah reached for a framed photo on the mahogany bedside table. "Happy 80th birthday to us both!" Sally had scribbled on the picture. "Enjoy my visible decay!"

Deborah studied the photograph and marveled at how well those incredible Greta Garbo cheekbones had survived. Even now in old age, despite the hooded eyes and the spidery lines radiating from Sally's lips. Yes now, even with the white hair reduced to a boyish cut and deep vertical crevices slashed into both cheeks, there remained an aloof loveliness about Sally, a kind of big-city elegance.

2014

Hi Deb,

Your letters lately have been on the picky-picky side. Okay, I have returned to upholding the trinity of Capitalization, Grammar, and Spelling, and no abbreviations. And what's more, next week I plan to board a train that makes a stop in Boxton! If you're still driving that pitiful Chevy Prizm which you so nauseatingly have described to me, and if you haven't yet donated it (or yourself) to the Salvation Army, you can collect me (British expression) at the station . . . assuming you have one out there in the wilds. Will arrive at 10:40 Wednesday morning.

Cheers, Sally

Despite her joy about the visit, Deborah felt embarrassed to bring the decrepit little Chevrolet to the Boxton station. Sally would certainly pass judgment on the automobile's badly corroded doors, fender dents, and sagging rear bumper. Deborah had been rear-ended three times. She never enjoyed driving even when she was much younger, especially with Aunt Tziporah sitting terrified in the passenger seat and her frequent Yiddish cries for help: *Oy gevaldt!*

Boxton had changed since those early days. The passing years yielded a horde of reckless drivers, who mocked Deborah's strict adherence to the speed limit. They blasted horns and shouted obscenities as they sped by. She identified the worst offenders as former problem children in her classes at Grammbly Elementary.

She was running late. To save time, she forced herself to use the frightening Interstate. She could see the shabby little station from the highway. With its dormers and old-fashioned window frames, it resembled the misshapen little houses her pupils once drew with their broken crayons.

After piloting the car into a convenient slot, she sighed and thanked her Creator for safe delivery. Sally arrived, dressed in skinny pants and a smock-like blouse that featured a single glittering green stripe against a pitch-black background. She wore a gold-colored scarf wrapped around her head in turban fashion, and she bounded off the train with the energy of a sixty-year-old.

"We have to delay lunch," she announced after the initial hugs and the pause while they surveyed what damage the passing years had done to their faces. "First, I demand a personal tour of your legendary little burg."

Still calling the shots, Deborah noticed. "Fine," she said. She didn't want to drive farther than she had to.

"But why Boxton? That's a good name for a container store." A wisecrack only Sally would make. Deborah ignored it.

"Folks here wanted privacy so they kept their yards separated with tall boxwood hedges. There was so much box the residents voted to change the town's name from Dunn's Back Pasture to Boxton."

Sally frowned. "Rather smug on their part."

"What do you mean?"

"Too self-satisfied. Why change a definitive name like Dunn's Back Pasture to glorify some monotonous bushes?"

Aware that Sally was teasing her again just as she had done in the old days, Deborah replied that she thought there was nothing wrong with calling the place Boxton.

Once started, Sally, as usual, wasn't abandoning the subject. "The way I see it, Deb, the world struggles with a variety of foliage sharing the same landscape. There are helpful hedges and hurtful hedges . . . and so . . ."

"I'm parked over here," Deborah said, waving her hand. The smudged cuff of her blouse protruded from the sleeve of her beige cardigan. Would Sally notice?

The Chevy Prizm had a difficult time getting started, but it finally hiccuped its way into traffic. Deborah made an awkward left turn at a blinking yellow traffic light, and they entered a side street of well-kept lawns. "We have some very nice homes here," she said. "There's an old saying in these parts: a hedge between keeps friendships green."

Sally frowned. "That sounds so limiting."

"Don't forget your seat belt," Deborah said in her best schoolteacher manner. Sally grinned and deliberately left it unbuckled. The car slowed to a crawl. Deborah felt she had to recharge the conversation, which seemed to be running uphill. "Boxton was originally called Dunn's Back Pasture because a man named George Dunn had a large dairy farm here. He raised Angus cows and sold milk and butter." She paused. "Also eggs."

Sally laughed. "You're telling me more than I want to know." She turned for a quick view of the back seat area where a strip of interior insulation sagged from the ceiling. "When does this carriage turn into a pumpkin?" she asked. "Or has it done that already?"

Same old Sally. Deborah smiled politely as she kept her eyes glued to the road. "Late model cars are not for me," she said. "They have scary electronic doodads that even talk back to you. I'd never remember how to handle all the flashing lights on the dashboard. Just too complicated."

"Read the manual."

"The print is too small."

A gloomy cloud of silence settled over the two friends. "Never got a license," Sally said after a long pause. "In Manhattan you don't need a car."

"Really? I learned at sixteen. One of my aunt's customers taught me." Oops, Deborah thought, I shouldn't have mentioned Aunt Tziporah. That could lead to answering painful questions about Steve. It could dampen Sally's long-delayed visit, which was beginning to seem pointless anyway. "This is Main Street," Deborah said. "That old red brick building over there used to be the elementary school where I taught." She shook her head, remembering. "Fifty years."

"Holy moly, Deb! Didn't we just pass Topiary Towers?"

"Yes. You can look forward to a grand tour of it after lunch."

"Sort of creepy, don't you think? All those grotesque creatures on the lawn. Are they for real?"

"They're pruned boxwood trees. Topiaries." Deborah found it difficult to concentrate on both steering the car and responding to this latter-day version of Sally, who still resembled her earlier self, only with more wrinkles.

"Horticultural zombies," Sally mumbled.

Deborah couldn't manage a clever defense and drive at the same time. "No, they're mostly animals—dogs and bunnies and things."

"Overdone, don't you think? Not subtle. I mean, no comparison to the classical 'scaping in France or Italy. If you weren't scared to death of getting on an airplane, you'd enjoy Montalto Pavese. It's an eighteenth-century garden that overlooks the Po Valley between Genoa and Milan. Lots of boxwood framing the flowerbeds. You would love it."

"Maybe."

"What?"

"Maybe I would."

"Deb, it's okay. Just focus on the road. There's a monster of a truck behind you. I think he wants to pass you. Watch it! Watch it!" Deborah quickly pulled the car over to a nearby curb and parked until the truck faded out of sight. "I may stop driving soon anyway," she said in a faint voice.

Sally leaned back against the threadbare seat and exhaled. "Good idea."

They remained quiet while Deborah pulled into a full-service station. She softly tooted the horn for assistance. "I never use those do-it-yourself pumps," she said. "Can't stand the smell of gasoline. Don't want to get any on my hands or clothes. I really miss the old-time filling stations, don't you?"

"I told you I don't drive."

"Right."

Service was slow. The two women waited in silence as a sullen teenage girl in cutoff jeans filled the tank. "I haven't been here in months," Deborah said. "Remember all those long gas lines back in the 1970s?"

Sally removed her wire-framed glasses and replaced them with an oversized pair of sunglasses. "I hope you haven't made any elaborate lunch reservations for today," she said. "I just have time to grab fast food somewhere, catch up with you a bit, and get back home. I have plans for tonight and you probably have too, don't you?"

"No."

"Don't give me your horrified this-is-the-end-of-civilization-as-we-know-it look. I remember it from college. Look, I promise to stay longer next time. Some day in the barren future you'll never get rid of me."

Deborah forced herself to keep the conversation going, but Sally didn't hear her. "Hey, Deb," she said, "you and I ought to go into the old-age home business. We could exploit the hell out of our fellow seniors. There's gold in them thar hills. Also in them thar pills."

"I don't live at an old-age home. It's an independent living facility."

"Same difference." Sally pretended to be lost in her original thought. "We could make a fortune. We'll call our business Graying Temples." She laughed. "By the way, I'm going to stop coloring my hair. Hell with it. It doesn't fool anybody."

Deborah couldn't think of a reasonable answer. "Topiary Towers was built in the late 1890s, but it has been completely renovated inside," she said. "We have a beautiful social hall and a fitness room with three Nu-Step machines and a treadmill, which I use every morning."

Wrestling with a handle on the door at her side, Sally struggled to open a window, gave up, and countered, "I take walks along the Hudson every day with my friend Ben Levy. I've written you about him, haven't I?"

"No." Deborah didn't care to discuss her friend's latest conquest. "This entire street of Victorian houses has been declared a Historic Preservation District. You should see it in the spring when the cherry blossoms are out."

Sally rarely permitted introduction of new topics unless she initiated them. "Surely I've mentioned Ben to you," she continued. "He's retired, was living full-time on a cruise ship, but now he's a landlubber and comes to New York frequently. Always stays at my place. Wants to move in with me, but I'm not wild about the idea." Deborah remained wordless, and Sally added, "Didn't you know about Ben and me?"

For goodness sake, Deborah thought, it was exactly the kind of wild thing Sally would do even at death's door, flirt shamelessly, shack up with every old reprobate she met. "No," Deborah said in a barely audible voice, "you haven't written or phoned in a couple of centuries."

Sally pretended she didn't hear. "He sat next to me at a Bartók concert, and we struck up an insane conversation. Before leaving, we exchanged phone numbers and addresses. It won't surprise you to learn that Ben is Jewish," she said. "Remember how back in college we Catholic girls always said that Jewish men made the best husbands?"

"Not always," Deborah wanted to say, but didn't. It could provoke unwanted questions from Sally, who still knew nothing much about Steve, other than the fact that things didn't work out. Deborah preferred to keep it that way.

"You know, my ex passed eleven years ago," Sally said in a matter-of-fact voice. "Poor Bill suffered from cirrhosis of the liver."

The casual tone surprised Deborah; she never liked Bill Hadley and didn't know how to answer. "Too bad," she said weakly. Sally appeared to be waiting for similar information volunteered in exchange, possibly some tidbit about Deborah's failed marriage. Not supplying any further information about Steve gave Deborah a rare sense of delicious superiority. She preferred to keep it that way. Besides, it was ancient history.

She piloted the car into the parking lot of a deserted Kentucky Fried Chicken emporium at the edge of town. "We'll eat inside," she said. "It's not elegant, but clean. Usually."

With a stiff nod she greeted the plump middle-aged cashier behind the counter. "That's Lois," Deborah whispered. "I held her back a year. She was a slow learner."

Sally pretended to be shocked. "I'll remember to count my change," she said. They ordered and carried their food to the nearest empty table. Sally resumed her end of the faltering conversation. "One reason I don't want Ben to move in with me is I may be leaving town and taking a full-time job elsewhere."

"I can't believe someone like you would say goodbye to New York."

"Well, someone like *you* may not have noticed that magazines and newspapers are dying off fast these days. Subscriptions have dropped, advertising is down to nothing. Just when female journalists started to get equal pay. Competition is the pits. My markets have dried up."

It was not a subject Deborah wanted to pursue, but at least it kept them talking to each other. "Come to think of it," she said in an obliging way, "I did wonder why the *Boxton Banner* closed its doors last spring. It had been family-run for a hundred and two years."

Sally wiped grease from her fingers with a paper napkin. "These days people get their news elsewhere. Print media is kaput." Sally tried to snap her long, manicured fingers to emphasize her point, but made no sound. "You know, Deb," she added, "we could communicate better if you didn't have this phobia about using social media."

"I value my privacy," Deborah answered mechanically.

Sally had retained her cosmopolitan way of speaking, half-mocking, self-confident, a cool tone which Deborah wished she could duplicate but never could get right. "There's one advantage to living as long as you and I have, Deb. It gives us time to mourn the housewives of our generation, the ones who burned themselves out in service to everybody but themselves."

Sally was galloping ahead at high speed, Deborah thought, and there would be no stopping her now.

"Betty and Gloria, bless 'em, I marched with all those second-wave feminists. But meanwhile, I was good enough to break the mold on my own. And looking back, so what? So I battled for underpaid female news hens, slaving away for chickenfeed. Things got a little better for us. But not much." Sally gestured as if to brush away the past. "Hell, who cares what I did years ago?"

"I do."

Sally gave her a tolerant smile. "I could tell you I've had drinks with Maureen O'Hara or Margaret Chase Smith or even Mother Machree, and you'd believe me, wouldn't you?"

"Always," Deborah said.

"Thanks. These days everybody else seems to lie. Plagiarism crops up more than you know. But somewhere a writer leaves a digital trail that wipes out falsehood. Too many paths to follow these days. It's a labyrinth leading to little truth and no consequences."

Deborah didn't care for conversations like this. "I guess so," she said.

"So, changing the subject, what mayhem goes on at the waxworks these days."

"What?"

"You know. Your Topiary Towers, Tomb of the Tottering and the Timid. Who was it who said, 'Of the making of old people there is no end?'"

"You did."

Sally gave a loud, harsh laugh and then softened her voice. "Seems to me you've been retired for an eternity. These days you must be glad you're not involved in the current debacle they call public education. Are you? Or aren't you?"

Surprised at the questioning, Deborah nodded and swore she didn't miss her job one bit. Why dip into lost worlds? Two years after she began teaching, the school became officially integrated, followed by years of protests by white parents, some of whom switched their children to private academies or home schooling. And now for the past two decades Grammbly Elementary no longer even existed. The original ninety-five-year-old brick building had been torn down, replaced by a Walmart. Students caught the bus to a consolidated regional school fifteen miles away. But what was all that to Sally?

"I do keep busy," Deborah said. "When I packed up to move from my house, I came across an old magazine from the 1950s and decided to keep it as a memento of times past. These days I spend a lot of time just reading and enjoying it."

Sally choked on a piece of chicken, coughed it up, and emptied her water glass with two hard swallows. "That's odd," she gasped. "Why waste your time on that?"

Deborah bravely forged ahead. "I mean, old magazines tell us so much about who we were and where the country was headed. As a journalist, you would really appreciate reading all the predictions that never came true."

"What's worse is all the things that did." Sally broke into another coughing spell; she searched her handbag for a lozenge. When she could answer audibly, she added, "Back in the day, we were indestructible. Who expected the Fifth Estate to fold?"

"Yes, hard to believe," Deborah said, not knowing what else to answer. She considered one last try. She wanted to reach across the table and touch the hand of her friend. She wanted to say, "Actually, my old magazine brings back fond memories of you." No, Sally would consider that too sentimental. Too icky. Perhaps she would take it personally and feel insulted, as if she herself were being compared to an outdated magazine, past its prime. Instead, Deborah raised the question, "Don't you miss our old favorites like *Woman's Home Companion* and *Ladies' Home Journal*?"

Sally frowned. "Why shed tears for them when the best newspapers and magazines in the world are breathing their last? And what's left except online garbage?"

"I wouldn't know," Deborah said, "I don't keep up much with current events."

Both silent, they concentrated on eating. On their way to the train station, Sally joked, "I'll let you pick up the bill when we eat at a fancier place next time."

"Which," Deborah replied dutifully, "I hope will be soon."

"Be careful what you wish for," Sally said.

No immediate visits followed. Deborah didn't expect any. Two years later, a startling letter arrived, announcing a new direction in Sally's life.

2016

Hi Deb,

Still living precariously! Last year I joined the editorial staff of the *Northwestern Shore Chronicle* and moved to the little town of Scarpville. Our editor, another expat from Manhattan, was delighted to hire this unemployed octogenarian because I work cheap. My young office mates (all two of them) have dubbed me a role model, but what do they know? I'm covering local high school basketball games, Bible study bashes, and interviews with the scrappy characters who abound in these parts. Hometown newspapers are our only salvation. We little guys boost local causes and describe what the hell is going on down the street. If readers object, they let us know in language that would shock you down to your Red Cross oxfords. (Do you still wear those?) One of these days, nevertheless, you and I will get together for another grand reunion, I solemnly swear.

Love, Sally

Although Deborah responded with effusive congratulations, she had trouble swapping her friend's old image for the ill-fitting new one. The world traveler had come down in the world. What could Sally find exciting about Main Street? Now there would be no more New York phone calls peppered with objections to the proposed tunnel under the Hudson River or mentions of Twyla Tharp's latest lifetime award or Sally's ongoing condemnation of *Cats*.

That autumn, a brief note jotted on a Jewish New Year's card arrived at Topiary Towers. "L'Shona Tova!" Sally scribbled beneath a color photo of apples and pomegranates. "Yes, my child, I've moved back to Manhattan. A voracious hedge fund bought our little newspaper; and no surprise, the damn leeches bled it to death in no time. Be aware I may appear before your eyes sooner than you think. Love, S."

Another of Sally's unkept promises, Deborah thought, but if the time did come, she would be prepared. She swore to herself never again to waste their precious hours together on small talk. She would pull her neglected skills out of mothballs. In a well-worn loose-leaf notebook, she outlined a massive lesson plan with a no-nonsense title:

Conversation Ideas Unit: Part 1

She would begin with a touch of humor. "Today, Class, we'll enjoy Show and Tell," she'd announce. "I'll go first." Before Sally could utter a cynical word, Deborah would haul out The Magazine. "Look what I brought!" she'd say in the same excited tone she once had used with her first graders. And for once, her friend would be speechless, and for once, Deborah would do all the talking. She could feel it in her varicose veins that the day would arrive, but she didn't know exactly when.

2017

The phone call was short and enigmatic. "Hi Deb," Sally said in a faint voice, "the magic moment is here. Look for me next Thursday, 10:00 a.m., at Boxton train station."

Although Deborah sensed turmoil lying in wait, she felt ready. When Sally arrived, she looked harried. In defiance of the summer heat, she wore a bulky black velvet dress, heavy and ankle-length. On her head sat a warped straw sunhat, on her feet brown and white lace-up granny boots. Her long gray hair hung limply against her cheek, and she was not smiling as she hobbled off the train with the help of the conductor.

Her first words were, "You're not still driving that Wreck of the Hesperus, are you?"

"I may get rid of it soon," Deborah said. "The door on the driver's side won't open, so I always have to get in first through the other door and slide across the front seat. It's a little uncomfortable passing over the handbrake."

"Be glad you're no longer a virgin," Sally mumbled, and then added, "You're not, are you?"

Deborah chose to ignore that remark. "It's good to see you," she said.

"Yeah." They walked in silence toward the Kiss and Ride Zone where the debilitated Prizm was parked. "This town looks like a haven for people who go around whistling all the time," Sally said. "Hey, Deb, you haven't heard me whistle in years." She jammed two bony forefingers into the corners of her mouth and emitted three ear-piercing notes. At that point, she lost her balance and would have fallen if Deborah hadn't grabbed her arm.

"My car door is still broken. I'll get in first, then you. And when we get to Cordelia's Tea House," Deborah said, "you get out first and then wait for me while I slide across the front seat."

"Since when are you so athletic?" Sally asked. Deborah felt she didn't have to answer that and said, "I made an 11:30 reservation for lunch to give us more time for catching up."

"I don't want the lousy fried chicken again."

"Cordelia serves delicious food. Her place is a fascinating old Victorian house bordering the Historic Preservation District."

Sally seemed to be on the verge of collapse as she struggled to close the dented car door behind her.

"Bang it hard. One more time ought to do it," Deborah said with a radiant smile. "No rush. It's so good to see you again. You're looking fit."

"For what?" Sally snarled, finally slamming the door shut.

After a strangely quiet ride of three short blocks, they arrived at their destination. With a definitive groan, Sally pulled herself out of the front seat.

"Just a minute, Sally," Deborah said after sliding over and exiting through the same door. "I have to lock the car."

"Who'd steal it?"

They inched their way along a precariously wet sidewalk, recently hosed down. "Almost there," Deborah said, "just take a few more baby steps." She tried to laugh. "Remember the game Mother, May I? The children used to love that."

Sally didn't care to answer. They passed a high boxwood hedge and approached the carved oak door of Cordelia's Tea House. "This is the fanciest restaurant in town," Deborah said. "Cordelia plays piano every day to entertain lunch customers. She was one of my pupils."

"Does this mean we get a free lunch?" Sally asked in a sour tone.

When they were comfortably seated at a table in a tiny lavender-painted alcove, Deborah knew it would be the perfect time to introduce her Lesson Plan. Instead, as Cordelia in the next room paid tribute to Rodgers and Hammerstein, Deborah distractedly babbled the first thought that entered her head. "I certainly do miss my own piano. When I moved, they couldn't fit it into my apartment."

"Can I get a Scotch and water in this flowery bower?" Sally gave her a belligerent look. "Just so you know, I've been off the wagon for the past month."

It was obvious at the train station, Deborah thought, although she wanted to pretend that her friend was on some new medication that hadn't agreed with her.

"Whatever will be, will be," Deborah answered, not knowing what else to say at that moment. "So, where was I? My piano. It was too big for the living room. I had to donate it to the nursery school."

"When did you get musical? You were always tone-deaf as hell." Sally motioned to a passing waitress. "Can I get a Scotch and water here?"

Deborah was determined to appear as unflappable as possible. "A teacher of young children has to be able to handle a piano. There was one in my classroom."

She paused. Just as she expected, wasted talk, useless palaver, even though they hadn't seen each other in such a long time. And Sally had the chutzpah to arrive in this condition. Deborah scolded herself for not recognizing it right away. One never knew with Sally.

"I'll have a Scotch and hold the water," Sally said to a passing waitress who wore a mutton-sleeved Gibson Girl blouse that badly needed ironing.

"Yes ma'am. Hi, Miz Greenbaum. What's yours?"

"Nothing, Mary Lou," Deborah said quickly. "I'm driving."

"If you can call it that," Sally muttered.

Deborah pretended not to hear. "May I recommend Cordelia's Chicken Caesar salad? It's tasty and very reasonable."

Sally heaved a weighty sigh and didn't respond.

Deborah convinced herself to remain sunny after the waitress hurried away. "I remember when Mary Lou gave chickenpox to twenty-five children in my class."

Sally shielded her left eye with a bony hand accented by artificial jade-green fingernails. "Last night I came in murderously late from a Mahler concert. I need a jolt today."

Mary Lou brought the drink, and they immediately fell into a silence that Deborah would have dreaded had she not done her homework. Smiling, she dug into her cavernous leather pocketbook to produce the plastic grocery bag in which she had stored her Show and Tell.

That morning while preparing for the big visit, Deborah had diligently followed her To-Do List for the day. She brushed her teeth, gargled with mouthwash, and dressed in a navy blue pantsuit that had seen better years. She swallowed her blood pressure pill, squirted drops into rheumy eyes, slathered foundation over the facial brown spots. She applied sunscreen and pale pink lipstick, packed her reading glasses and a credit card, mislaid her keys twice and located them in a frenzy. She even limited her liquid intake to avoid any bladder interruptions that could lie ahead. Her memory cooperated down to the tiniest detail, touching all bases, or so she thought.

As she rummaged through her pocketbook, Deborah developed a sinking ache in her stomach. She had left The Magazine on a pie-crust mahogany table in the entrance hall of her apartment. There would be no Show and only an improvised Tell.

Without reinforcement, Deborah took a desperate plunge. "Know what my hobby is these days, Sally?"

"Seducing the randy geezers at your old-age home?"

Deborah smiled. Same wicked old Sally. She had always been a heavy drinker at State U., but back then it seemed like a sophisticated tipsy part she once played in a college play. "No," Deborah said, "it may sound peculiar, but I'm fascinated by . . ." She took a deep breath . . . "old magazines."

Sally stared at her with glazed eyes. "And I'm interested in new ones, only they're few and far between these days." She raised her glass. "To oblivion," she said.

Deborah tried again. "Old magazines can be very interesting. I have a very old one. Later when we get back to my place, I'll show it to you."

But Sally went off the deep end. "Once when I gave a talk to a writers' group in the Hamptons, I began with a bang. Quoted Lord Byron." She took a hearty swallow of Scotch. "He wrote, 'Condemn'd to drudge, the meanest of the mean / And furbish falsehoods for a magazine.' That really got a rise out of those phonies."

"What does "furbish falsehoods" mean?

"Damned if I know."

Deborah soldiered on. "Speaking of magazines, know what surprises me? Many nineteenth-century magazines had such stuffy names. I mean, couldn't the men who published them come up with anything more interesting than their own last names? *McCall's, Harper's, Collier's.* Did you know there really was a Mr. McCall, a Mr. Collier?"

"Yes. So what?"

"Online I found a whole list of discontinued American magazines I never heard of."

"And they never heard of you."

Although Sally laughed too much at what she obviously considered a joke, Deborah pretended not to hear and continued. "Many magazine founders were immigrants. Like James McCall, a Scottish tailor, who arrived in 1873. He started a magazine just to sell dress patterns to women who sewed at home."

"Condemn'd to drudge, the meanest of the mean," Sally said. "I have to go to the ladies' room." Deborah didn't accompany her. She pitied her friend, but it wasn't dignified for a retired first grade teacher to be seen ushering an inebriated stranger to the toilet. Not at Cordelia's Tea House, anyway. When Sally returned, she shuffled, taking short stop-and-go steps as if her legs had ballooned en route.

"I meant to bring something to show you," Deborah said, "but at the last minute I forgot. It was an old magazine from the 1950s. A real collector's item. The ads in it are especially funny."

"Advertising. Or lack thereof. That's what clobbered the best magazines in the business." Sally tilted her glass to capture the last drop. "How 'bout a refill? Another Sprite?"

Deborah shook her head. The sound of the piano continued from the next room. "Cordelia was always musical," she said. "In my class I remember she would sing 'Oh! Susannah' louder than anybody else. But instead of 'I come from Alabama with a banjo on my knee,' she changed it to 'with a band-aid on my knee.'"

Sally didn't laugh, and Deborah continued. "I'm not a musician. But I could manage simple tunes for the children." Deborah felt proud that she had at least one talent that Sally lacked. "I even once composed an original song for my class."

"Made it up yourself? Music and lyrics? Where the hell is the waitress?" Sally waved to Mary Lou, pantomimed drinking a shot of whiskey, and turned back to Deborah. "You wrote a song? I'm flabbergasted."

"It was about giraffes," Deborah said, almost apologetic.

"Giraffes! The crazy horses dressed up in pajamas? No, wait, that's zebras. But, hey Deb, didj'ever write a sonata about those horny gorillas in Africa? I met Jane Goodall at a party once." Sally raised her most recent Scotch and water. "Here's to my good friend Deb, a warbling environmentalist out to save the world."

"Not exactly," Deborah mumbled.

Sally emptied her glass and pounded a blue-veined fist on the table. "Let's hear your song!"

"Not here. Another time." Deborah pretended to smile at Mary Lou as she passed, eyes rolling.

"I insist! Command performance!"

Deborah felt the old shyness coming on. She thought she had abandoned that discomfort years ago. "No, I don't think Cordelia would approve."

"We'll have a sing-along. Hey, Cornelia, get that piano in here!" Sally yelled, enjoying herself. She turned to focus again on Deborah. "What's the name of your little ditty?"

"*Giraffe Jive.*"

"Jive? *Giraffe Jive?*"

"One of my pupils suggested the title."

Sally started to laugh and couldn't stop.

"He was only six years old," Deborah said as if she were begging forgiveness. "The first Black child I ever taught."

Sally quickly emptied her glass, rose to her feet, clapped her hands, and announced in a voice loud enough for Cordelia to hear in the next room:

"Ladies and Gentlemen! The internationally famous environmentalist, educator, and composer Deborah Greenbaum sings her immortal *Giraffe Jive*! You're on, kid."

Deborah stared down at her lap and hoped her friend would simmer down. Boxton, for heaven's sake, wasn't New York City. Back in college days, she never liked it when Sally publicly teased her, but that was years ago, and now it had all come back in adult strength. "C'mon," Sally pleaded, "c'mon, Deb."

Embarrassed, yet somehow still eager to please, Deborah began in a small, uncertain voice: "Giraffes are skinny / And quite tall / They always make me grin / Their throat's so long, / Their food gets lost / And that's why they're so thin. / I wish giraffes were fatter . . . and small."

Sally applauded loudly. "Encore! Encore! Another song and another drinkie! Where the hell is Mary Lou?"

"I haven't written anything else since," Deborah said.

"Did all the little buggers like it?"

Deborah cringed, hoping that no one nearby could overhear. "At PTA meetings, parents said they remembered learning it in my class. I'm told kindergarteners and first graders still sing it."

"It has more depth than 'Eeensy Weensy Spider,'" Sally said with no expression on her face. "Another Sprite, Deb?"

Deborah shook her head. She glanced around the room. The nearest tables were empty. A blessing.

"Judgmental Deborah. Wasn't there a Deborah in the Old Testament? A federal judge of some kind?" Sally didn't wait for an answer. "You've always been the cautious one," she said mournfully. "If I'd followed your lead, maybe I wouldn't have messed up."

"You've had a good career."

"Should've gone into television."

"You were attractive enough."

"Never knew what end was up. You did. Always satisfied with whatever."

"Not always." Nobody, Deborah thought, lives almost nine decades and doesn't wish some things might have been different. She didn't elaborate. Why make the conversation gloomier than it was turning out to be?

Sally fell into a brooding silence until Mary Lou brought her a refill.

"A toast!" Sally raised her glass, trying to keep her balance as she stood up. "To jivin' giraffes and expirin' print news and publishers who boot talent out the door . . . and . . . and . . . while we're at it, here's to all the sunken vessels at the bottom of the sea!" She finished her drink with a triumphant Irish smile. Deborah sighed. There was no way to rescue the conversation now.

Sally continued. "Hey Deb, did I ever tell you Dad was in the Navy? He always called me 'Skipper.' An' later, Skip for short. Big brother Bob called me Skip, too. We lost Bob in Vietnam, but let's not jump into that cesspool right now."

It was the first time Deborah ever heard this. She felt like saying, "I'm so sorry, Skip," but it seemed inappropriate after all these years. Besides, she didn't dare call Sally "Skip." That would be invading her privacy, using a pet name given her by family. And anyway, World War Two and Vietnam seemed too heavy a load for a casual lunch at Cordelia's Tea House.

Before Deborah could think of an appropriate answer, Sally took the helm again. "Know what?" she lowered her voice to a whisper. "I have conversations out loud with myself." She paused. "Ever do that?"

"It's okay to talk to yourself," Deborah said charitably, "if you don't do it in public."

They pretended to busy themselves with their Caesar salads. Deborah thought that any further discussion would be too sad or too frightening or too something.

Sally glanced at her watch. "Don't let me miss the train. Marty Feinberg has tickets for something or other tonight. He's the new man in my life."

Why, Deborah wondered, hadn't Sally planned the Boxton visit for a more convenient time? "So soon? You just got here. Can't I offer you a cup of tea in my apartment? At least a Little Debbie?"

"Next time around." Sally's voice sounded confident now, more like her younger self. "You're such a worrywart. I'll get home all right." She grinned. "You know me and my hollow leg from way back."

At the train station, they hugged, and Sally headed for Manhattan; Deborah drove home to the swollen boxwood creatures waiting for her on the lawn at Topiary Towers. For the first time she saw them as bloated imposters with no logical reason to exist. She had read somewhere that people could order do-it-yourself topiary plans for creating their own outsized freaks. The leafy banality of their existence reminded her of the paint-by-numbers landscapes available at the local art supply shop.

She haltingly backed into the numbered space allotted to her in the residents' parking lot. She pulled up the handbrake, removed the ignition key, and sat for a few minutes to recover from the strain of driving.

The visit from Sally left Deborah with uneasy questions. How should she evaluate it? Where was the substance? What was the point? The two of them behaved as if nothing significant ever happened to them over their lifetimes, at least nothing worth talking about. But their friendship had survived too many years to shrivel and die without a struggle. She was certain that the living spark between them may have dimmed but it hadn't flickered out. Deborah swore to herself that next time they met she would not forget to bring The Magazine. She would target certain favorite parts to make Sally laugh. They would grow close again, the two of them together. And maybe they would cry a little together, too, as they remembered.

2019

Two winters passed before Sally took it upon herself to call. "Hey Deb, would you believe we've been hit by a blizzard?" she said. "Gotham has shut down completely."

"I know," Deborah said, "I watch the Weather Channel. Are you okay?"

Sally didn't answer immediately, and when she did her words sounded memorized from earlier apologies. "I've been such a rotten friend not to answer all your messages. But we'll get together soon. If you let me, I'll come visit you and even spend the night. That's a promise."

"I'll believe it when I see it," Deborah said. "You told me you were on your way last October and you never came. I called. I wrote. Just couldn't reach you."

"Deb, if we live long enough, there's hope for us. Have you heard that eighty-five is the new sixty-five?"

"In case you've lost count, we're eighty-seven."

"Just so you know," Sally paused for breath, "I've survived Rehab. Surprise!

I'm cold sober these days." Then she turned almost childlike. "But I guess by now you and I are kaput. I always thought we'd be friends till hell freezes over. Do you think you'd ever want to put up with the likes of me again?"

Deborah felt tears stinging her eyes. "Always, Sally." And she thought, here we go again.

"Mission accomplished. I'll see you when the swallows come back to Capistrano. They're preparing for a soft landing."

Although Deborah didn't quite know what that meant, she was pleased that Sally still liked to wrap herself in drama. Perhaps this time would be worth the wait.

2020

In the stale air of her living room at Topiary Towers, Deborah shifted her body on the faded maroon recliner and tried to find a position that would not aggravate her spinal vertebrae. The ventilation was poor because she had never been strong enough to open any windows in the apartment. The TV was turned on, but these days she muted it and closed her eyes to avoid the ominous headlines on the evening news programs: Physicians Warn of Covid-19 Risks, Clinical Trials Must Back Treatments; Doctors Say, Sun Belt Nursing Homes Not Ready for Shutdown Against Virus; A Thousand Deaths a Day, Efforts Falter to Bring Down Community Transmission; Fighting Virus, Science Lacks Evidence; Covid Hits Pregnant Latinas Hard; ER Nurse Asks "Am I Next?"

Deborah napped briefly, but it was too early to go to bed. Opening her eyes, she studied a framed photograph mounted on the opposite wall. It was an enlarged black-and-white snapshot of her father conducting a Passover Seder, her dark-eyed mother seated next to him. Deborah sighed. She never had known them or heard their voices. Her mood changed when she glanced at the studio portrait of a youthful Steve, his hair slicked down with pomade, his cheeks tinted a soft pink. Now more than six decades later, she could hear Aunt Tziporah's querulous voice demanding, "Why save a picture of that low-life bum?"

"Not the point," Deborah said aloud to no one in particular. She prided herself on keeping a record of things. In bulging scrapbooks, she included lists of favorite pupils, those who had been her best readers over the years, those who continued as adults to Be Somebody. On lonely evenings she enjoyed reading their names and tried to remember their faces. The former president of the Boxton Historical Society once introduced her as "Our archivist and official hoarder of times past."

Deborah deliberately avoided erasing Steve from her memory. In no way did she miss the dismal sex part, blessedly short-lived and painful even before the hysterectomy. Perhaps she continued to keep his picture handy because, like taking a multivitamin pill, he somehow was good for her health. Each time she saw his vulgar face, she relived the pleasure of having gotten rid of him.

She adjusted the recliner to a sitting position and finished reading a newspaper article about the difficulty of conducting classes online during the pandemic. Virtual learning they called it. As she studied the complaints of teachers who had to deal with it each day, her compassion mingled with a sense of overwhelming relief. Thank God I retired in time, Deborah thought. Rarely the victor in battles with her demonic computer, she wouldn't have been able to accomplish anything with her pupils. She felt almost smug, being safely out of it, above and beyond the electronic morass, the futility of teaching her six-year-olds how to read. And . . . and . . . she would not let herself even think of those horrific school shootings she often read about in the paper.

It was time for her last glass of water for the day. In her flip-flopping chenille house slippers, Deborah trudged to the kitchen, never once glancing at the hallway mirror. These days she wasn't eager to see that stoop-shouldered, white-haired person who frowned at her each time she passed. At the sink she filled a measuring cup with eight ounces of tap water. Down the hatch, she whispered to herself, counting each swallow.

During those lonely weeks of Covid quarantine, The Magazine remained her closest companion. Sometimes she imagined that she and Sally had become models and hired themselves out to pose as housewives in advertisements for vacuum cleaners and scented bar soap promising "the skin you love to touch." Or she shook her head in disapproval over the debut of a miraculous toothpaste now long departed from the market. The bombastic full-page ad read:

"Unforgettable Medical Moments: (1) Jenner's smallpox vaccination in 1796. (2) Fleming discovers penicillin in 1929. (3) NOW—1956—the latest triumph in toothpaste . . . VICTORY OVER DECAYING TEETH."

How trivial, Deborah thought. Who could imagine all these years later that we would again face a real plague that touches millions? No one is safe now except Sally, who, no doubt as an aware journalist, had the presence of mind to hop a freighter just in time and flee to some uncharted Pacific island. Most likely by now she had attracted an exotic man with a massive beard, living with him in a straw hut where she is writing the great American novel of the twenty-first century. Deborah caught herself. Not even Sally would be that risky. These days it wasn't safe for anyone their age to travel by plane or boat.

But The Magazine, Deborah's prized possession, never went anywhere. It stayed home on the closet shelf unless she took it down to keep her company. She did this repeatedly except for that one heartbreaking evening when she fell asleep with it on her lap. It had slipped out of sight, hidden between the maroon recliner and the wall. Exhausted, she left it there and headed for bed. And the next day Marie-Elana tossed it down the garbage chute. Kaput, in Sally's words. Surely, by now it had been reduced to ashes at the county landfill.

Night after night Sally's face came to Deborah in her dreams. Where was she now? The dehydrated, colorless hours of quarantine continued at Topiary Towers. Every morning Deborah called New York even though she knew a mechanical voice on the other end of the line would declare Sally's phone number no longer in service. Perhaps she had just returned from a long assignment somewhere and was too busy catching up on neglected matters to bother reconnecting the phone. That's probably what happened. Or even more likely, she had discontinued the landline in favor of one of those horribly complicated smartphones, and she simply forgot to give Deborah the new number. Although that made sense, her anxiety continued to grow. Each evening she crafted letters in the splendid cursive handwriting that she had learned as a child. Her plaintive message always ended with, "Sally, I hate not hearing from you. Please write or call." Sally did neither.

Concentration became a chore. Days slipped away; Deborah couldn't focus, couldn't read or watch television. She mailed one final handwritten note to

Sally's postal address, and this time, five envelopes came back, stamped "Return to Sender."

Deborah felt a numbing loneliness filling every cell of her body. She could no longer relax on the dependable maroon recliner. If she remained too long lying in one place, the slightest flex of calf muscle produced an excruciating cramp in her left leg. There was nothing to do but ease herself to a standing position, drink eight ounces of water, and then walk back and forth, breathing deeply, hoping the pain would recede. For distraction, she spun a fuzzy lesson plan in her head.

1. Objective: To discover where Sally had gone.
2. Desired Result: Knowledge of why she remained out of touch.
3. Application of Knowledge. That was the hardest part. What came next? And then what?

Later at night in bed, Deborah found no position that satisfied her twisting body. She snuffed out another intense leg cramp by inhaling deeply, holding her breath to a count of three, exhaling slowly to the count of ten. The glow of streetlights illuminated the silent topiaries on the lawn below her bedroom window. Deborah hobbled to her desk, switched on the light. Sally, where have you wandered this time? There's no one I can ask, Deborah thought. She sat frozen at the computer.

For weeks she had been avoiding this search. She pressed a key, entered her friend's name, added the brutal word "obituary," and found what she had hoped not to see. The cold digital letters materialized on the website of a New York crematorium. "Sally Harrigan Hadley. Died April 10, 2020, of Covid-19 complications."

No, Deborah moaned. The word stuck in her throat. She dragged herself to the window and stared at the monster foliage on the lawn of Topiary Towers. No, she whispered to the swollen green animals rising from the grass. No, she shouted to those useless distortions of leaves and boughs, the horticultural zombies, mute and indifferent to her pain, but still bursting with more life than Sally would ever see again.

Deborah shook her head to combat the anger that caused her heart to beat more rapidly than ever before. Somebody lied. The truth, where did it go? Some officials swore the virus was a myth, an Aesop fable with no moral. It all would disappear like magic, they promised. Even from the beginning, they knew how dreadful it was, but they didn't say. And she believed every lie because she wanted to. Let's pretend, boys and girls. Surely the disease would be no match for a free spirit like Sally, she thought. But it didn't work that way. The scourge had robbed Sally of her breath, her elegance, her loveliness.

Four bedroom walls seemed to waltz around Deborah; the ceiling tilted, the floor see-sawed beneath her feet. To steady herself, she reached for a corner of the nearby night table. The sudden movement shook Sally's photo, and it made no sound as it slid to the floor. When she bent to retrieve it, she thought about calling someone for help but what good would it do? She staggered into the hallway leading to the kitchen and saw on the wall the faces of her young parents, now forever silent, erased by the torture of diphtheria. Her sense of order urged her to reach out not only to them but to unremembered souls lost in each relentless pestilence since the beginning of time.

And then as Deborah wept for them all, quietly so that her neighbors would not be disturbed, she accepted the final truth about herself and Sally. They had frittered away too many years. Their one remaining chance to turn the pages would not return. They would never again share the remnants of their youth nor the affirmation of their old age.

EPILOGUE

Weeks later, still drained by her loss, Deborah received an email from a user address she didn't recognize. She automatically deleted such electronic intruders, but this time her trembling fingers touched another computer key quite by accident. A startling message flashed on the screen.

Hello Ms. Greenbaum,

The ashes of my mother, Sally Harrigan, were scattered to the four winds last week. We attended her brief ceremony on the shore of the Chesapeake Bay, just my brother Sean and me. Because of Covid, we were not allowed to say goodbye to her at the hospital. She passed away with no one at her bedside.

I've been finding old letters handwritten by you to my mom during the years after the two of you finished college. She kept them stashed away in a carry-on bag that she left at our grandparents' house. It's an odd piece of luggage with Egyptian hieroglyphics sketched into beige leather. She must have bought it when she was covering stories in Cairo.

As you may know, my brother and I were adopted by my grandparents and raised by them. When she wasn't on assignment, my mother tried to remain in touch with us, but she never enjoyed the intensity of family life. As kids, Sean could take her or leave her, but I never got along with Sally. On our strained occasions together, mainly Christmas and Easter, we disagreed about everything. She often spoke of you. There were times I felt jealous because she praised you as much as she pilloried me.

Studying her correspondence, I'm struck by her devotion to her longtime friends all over the world. Belonging as she did to a military family, it was part of her heritage, adapting to new horizons and new faces. From my sailor grandfather, she inherited the skill of living meaningfully among strangers. She found a oneness with them. They meant more to her than her own children. Or at least I always thought so.

I would like very much to meet you in person because you were a part of her life more than I was. When I googled the place where you live, it said visitors weren't allowed now because of the Covid lockdown. If it's not too much to ask, let's get together after this dreadful nightmare ends.

Please find time for me; my mother never did. I want to learn more about her life, especially her youthful days. We moved to the States from Tel Aviv last year. My husband Alon and our bilingual children, Tamar and Lior, also want to know you. I'm so glad to have found you. My family loves to receive letters, especially in English. If you agree, let's correspond until better days return for us all.

Fondly, Meghan Hadley Ben-Zion

That night Deborah lost herself in dreams; Sally hovered nearby above a deserted beach. She wore a shirtwaist dress with a buttoned-down collar, the uniform of a 1950s housewife. Her waist was slim, her face unlined, her long red hair streaming down her back. She descended to the water's edge and scooped a handful of white pebbles from the sand beneath her feet. She stood tall and hurled the stones one by one at the blinding sun overhead. The sky turned black, and the voice of Sally's youth sifted through the darkness.

"Hey, Deb," she called, "did you know that ninety is the new seventy?"

"If you say so."

"Would I lie to you?"

"Will one hundred and twenty be the new one hundred?" Deborah asked.

Sally's laugh dissolved into the spray of the misty Chesapeake. On the beach, the tide had left behind a message written in flowing cursive letters. The graceful script spelled out four words: *Go forth and behold!*

Then as an elegant white-capped wave touched the shore, Deborah woke. A smile was on her lips, and she promised herself to answer daughter Meghan's email first thing that morning.

Rockville, Maryland, 2022

SHORT STORIES

SUPERFROG

After her mother died, Amy dropped out of Heatherford Community College and deserted her father's suburban split-level for a shabby group house in town. She found a clerk-typist job at a small advertising agency. All day long she typed orders that purchased television and radio time from local stations. One afternoon in May, six months after the funeral, Amy threw up in the ladies' room and had to leave work early in a taxi.

Riding home in the cab, she remembered she hadn't returned the library copy of *Complete Poems of Emily Dickinson*. It was five weeks overdue, but she couldn't bring herself to part with it. "Tomorrow," she whispered to nobody.

At the brick duplex she shared with Troy and Margaret she dragged herself up the chipped stone steps, pushed open the front door, and climbed the splintery stairs to her second-floor bedroom. Inside, there was no air-conditioning, and the striped yellow wallpaper shimmered, rippling like a pool of hot yellow water. Her head ached with fever.

She collapsed on the box-spring mattress and dozed. And when she opened her eyes, she saw Emily Dickinson seated on the bridge chair at the foot of the bed.

At first Amy thought it was the hotel bath towel her father had brought her as a souvenir from his recent honeymoon trip. But no, it was surely Emily holding a sprig of white. "Honeysuckle," Amy said out loud. Her housemate Troy had cut some from a neighbor's back fence and carried it up to Amy's room the evening before.

Emily rose and hovered over the green and gold chenille bedspread. Her brown eyes might have been Amy's except that there was no mascara or black liner. What were they? "Like leftover sherry in the glass," Emily once wrote. Amy didn't know what color sherry was, but it sounded classier than saying you had eyes like a beer gone flat.

"So what do you think of Dr. Armstrong giving me an 'F' on the term paper I wrote about you for American Lit?" Amy asked. At the same time she was comparing her own oval face and slight build with Emily's. They looked amazingly alike.

Emily didn't speak. "I guess you know Heatherford Community College has a nothing library," Amy said. "Everybody else in our class got there before me and grabbed up all the books on you. That was the same time Mom was in the hospital and after we found out what she had, I couldn't leave her for two days." Emily nodded. "So to save time I copied some stuff from the encyclopedia word for word. I handed it in, and Armstrong called me to her office for a lecture. She wouldn't let me explain."

Amy felt the tears still frozen inside her, but they wouldn't melt. She hadn't cried even at the funeral. She glanced around her hot room bloated with May sunshine and thought, suppose her visitor wasn't Emily. Suppose she was just some boring ghost nobody ever heard of? All those Victorian women looked alike with their hair parted in the middle.

"Who are you really?" Amy asked.

"It's me," her housemate Margaret said. "You left the front door wide open. When did you get home?" She was short of breath from climbing the stairs. "What's the matter? You look awful."

A taller shape blocked the light. It was Troy, as skinny as Margaret was ample. Troy had dropped out of the state university and now sold vacation real estate over the phone. Lately, he talked about getting a job in Alaska.

"Do you hurt anywhere, Amy?" Margaret shouted in her basso voice.

"Flu," Troy diagnosed. "She never got it last winter when the rest of us did." He tugged at the hairs in his skimpy auburn beard. Amy had never seen him look so worried.

"Open the window, Troy," Margaret said as she automatically picked up a white towel from the floor. During the day she worked for Marvelous Maids, a team that cleaned houses, but by night she was a ceramics artist. Now she bent over Amy and pulled gently at her bedsheet. "Want water?" she asked.

Amy looked beyond Margaret's good-natured face to see if Emily had gone away. She hadn't. Her figure at the window was sharper now. She wore a long white piqué dress high at the neck and a batiste shawl crisscrossed under her collar. Her skirt was covered with eyelet embroidery like the summer half-slip Amy had left lying on top of the wicker hamper just under the window.

Amy closed her eyes and tried to remember the words to one of Emily's poems. "*After great pain*," she muttered, "*a formal feeling comes.*"

"Hot as a pistol," Margaret said, putting her plump hand on Amy's forehead. "Where did you say you have this pain?"

"Emily said it, not me."

"Call Dr. Brennan," Margaret said to Troy. "Leave a message."

Troy shifted toward the door. "Right. And I'll get the thermometer," he said. Amy could hear his athletic shoes thumping down the stairs. Margaret wiped sweat off Amy's nose.

"Sweetie," Margaret said, "don't you know you're keeping me from my work? I promised to make six frog statues to sell at the Summer Crafts Festival. Remind me to show you my all-frog version of the old Dutch Masters when you get better."

Amy thought her housemate made the best ceramic frogs in the world, all shining green and feisty. Margaret stared at Amy with a solemn expression and said, "Maybe we ought to call your father."

"Don't," Amy said. "He won't come. His new wife won't let him." Her father, the manager of a shoe store, had married Carol, who was a couple of years older than Amy. No, Amy said, she didn't want anything from her father.

"He'll come if I mention you're out of your head with fever," Margaret said.

Troy hurried into the room. "The doctor's on vacation," he said in a loud voice that didn't sound like him. "The answering service is trying to find his associate." He handed a thermometer to Margaret, who poked it under Amy's tongue. "Don't bite down," Troy said.

Amy pushed away the thermometer long enough to say, "Quiet, you'll scare her," and pointed in the direction of Emily standing in a far corner of the room.

Margaret thrust the thermometer back into Amy's mouth. Both she and Troy turned to look at the empty corner and then at each other. Margaret finished taking Amy's temperature and whistled. "Don't panic," she said. "I'll be right back. Troy, get the rubbing alcohol."

Amy was left again with Emily, who drifted over to the cement-block book-case Troy had built. Amy watched as her visitor ran a pale finger over two thick volumes. One was the overdue library book of Emily's poems, and the other was a faded *Big Golden Book* of children's verse.

"Your life must have been really neat," Amy whispered, "not having to go out anywhere, just staying home dressed in white and hanging baskets of cookies out the window for little kids."

Emily stood with her back to Amy and played with a moth that had entered through the torn window screen. Amy thought the fluttering made a grainy sound like somebody throwing sand.

"After Mom died," Amy said, "I went to Dr. Armstrong to see if I could improve my American Lit grade. Actually, that was part of it. I really wanted to talk about 'After Great Pain a Formal Feeling Comes.' Remember?"

A corner of Emily's batiste shawl swayed silently at the window along with two white nylon curtain panels flapping in a sudden breeze.

"I wanted to tell her I really understood that poem, all that business of feeling stiff, you know? Because the death of your mom makes you feel you're a robot. I liked the part about how your feet go around and around in a mechanical kind of way. They take you to the supermarket and classes even when you don't want to be there.

"But Dr. Armstrong was busy when I came to the office. The door was half open. I could hear her talking on the phone. She was really upset that the college had decided to cut back on her teaching hours."

Emily trapped the moth in her billowing white skirt.

"Then Dr. Armstrong said she had half a mind to either blow her brains out or go into computer programming. And she asked for some professor's address to write to for a job recommendation at another college. And then she said it would feel good to get away from all the pitiful creeps she had to teach at this place and their feeble excuses for not measuring up."

Amy licked her dry lips. "After that I was too tired to talk about your poem, Emily, or explain anything. I stood there thinking about what you once called 'the hour of lead.' And then I just left and didn't ever come back."

Little by little the room turned lavender. Shadows formed hard black puddles around the furniture. The moon through the nylon panels broke in two.

Emily stood staring out the window, which overlooked a back alley behind the row of houses on Flower Avenue. The street was just inside the city line.

Tiny backyards bordered the opposite sides of the alley, and each rectangle of grass was staked out with a heavy chain-link fence dripping honeysuckle.

Amy tried to view the scene through Emily's eyes. The yards didn't inspire much poetry. Parked next to a concrete access road were the trucks of dry cleaners and paperhangers who lived on the block. But it wasn't every inch concrete. You could still hear crickets from somewhere.

"Once when I was little," Amy said, "I heard crickets outside and I said to Mom, that must be the birds snoring. She sent it off to a magazine and got five dollars for it. She said she was so proud of me. She went out and bought me this *Big Golden Book of Poetry: 85 Childhood Favorites*. And then she read me a new poem every night before bed."

With a shaky hand Amy reached for the book. "Here's one of yours, Emily, remember? *"I'm nobody! Who are you? Are you nobody too?"* Amy's voice cracked. *"How dreary to be somebody. How public like a frog . . ."*

"What in the world are you doing over there?" Margaret said. She helped Amy back into bed and rushed out to find Troy. Amy squinted hard, trying to locate Emily's white dress in the darkening room.

Then a lamp was switched on near the bookcase and something huge blocked Amy's view. "Mom hoped I'd become a teacher," Amy said, stretching her neck to see beyond the barrier. Margaret plopped a dripping washcloth on Amy's forehead and rubbed her arms with alcohol.

"And take these," Margaret said. She held the aspirin and a waxy white paper cup to Amy's lips. The water dribbled down her chin onto her white batiste blouse. Margaret didn't go away. She pushed a hard green object into Amy's hand. "Here's something to cheer you up," she said. Amy strained, looking for Emily.

"It's Superfrog!" Margaret said. "See the cape and the S on his shirt? Superfrog to the rescue! A get-well present from me, Sweetie."

Amy examined the frog. It had a cocky expression as if it could conquer the world. "He doesn't look dreary, Emily," Amy said.

"This frog can leap over tall buildings in a single bound," Troy said. "He can do anything."

Emily drifted over to the bedside. She stared down at Amy, how long she couldn't say. Amy fell asleep waiting. She slept seconds or hours, and when she opened her eyes, Emily was still there. She appeared ready to say a few words.

Amy could hardly wait to hear. But when Emily parted her lips, it wasn't what Amy expected. She hoped for her mother's soft tones, soothing, full of smiles and love. But Emily's voice wasn't like that. It wasn't even poetic. No, not even human speech. More like the pulse of insect wings scraping in rhythm just under the window.

Now the tears came, sideways from Amy's eyes to her hairline. The skin on her cheek grew itchy from all the wetness. She sobbed hard, and above the sound Margaret was saying, "Amy, Troy will drive you over to the Emergency Room at Mercy Hospital. Can you stand up?" Someone was lifting Amy's legs and lowering them over the side of the mattress.

"Mom couldn't even talk on the respirator," Amy said, weeping quietly. "She printed big shaky letters, *turn it off, turn it off.* But when I asked the nurse, she wouldn't. She told me I should act braver and try to cheer Mom up instead. She died before I could think of any way to do that."

"Pass me her other shoe," Margaret said to Troy. "It's going to be tricky getting her down the steps."

"All those tubes sticking into her," Amy said. "How could I pretend nothing was wrong? Her eyes looked so scared." Margaret gripped Amy's right arm and Troy took the other. Amy glanced up. Now Margaret was draping a white Orlon sweater around Amy's shoulders. Emily soared by in a rush of white.

"You're doing just great, Sweetie," Margaret said as they guided her toward the bedroom door. "I'm proud of you."

"Me too," Troy said.

"And so is Superfrog. Because he's a frog of steel," Margaret said. "And he'll pull you through easy as pie."

"Faster than a speeding bullet," Troy said, smiling at Amy, whose knees buckled under her. "Lean on me. I won't let you fall."

"Troy," Amy whispered, "don't run away to Alaska."

"No way," he said gently. "Watch the steps. Take it easy."

"Go back to school and finish."

"I'll think about it. One step. Another step. Almost there."

"And when I get better," Amy said. "I'm going back too. When you see my mom, Emily, tell her what I decided. It will really cheer her up, don't you think?"

They had reached the bottom of the stairs now. Troy yanked open the front door, and Amy could feel a rush of cool air. "You will tell her, won't you?" Amy asked and looked over her shoulder for Emily's answer, but she had already disappeared into a May night noisy with snoring birds and wild with honeysuckle.

PIANO BLUES

Jim said, "Mother thinks we ought to wait."

"She never opened her mouth," I said. "Not to me anyway."

"You know Mother. She doesn't like to butt in."

I let that pass. "If we want to buy Amy a piano, it's our business."

"A good piano costs. Besides, Amy's only eight."

"She has talent. The teacher in school says so."

Jim's mother came into the kitchen for her morning cup of tea. She smiled at Jim. She nodded grimly in my direction. I fled to get dressed.

Jim was home from work for the holiday. We wanted to get to the store early for the George Washington Birthday Sale. Jim's mother stayed behind. Jim said she didn't want to meddle. You could have fooled me.

We went to a store that advertised bargains on secondhand pianos. I liked one with curlicues that reminded me of wooden carousel horses. Jim said we shouldn't go overboard on price like that.

"Suppose Amy doesn't stick to it," he said. "Why invest a lot until we know for sure?"

His mother had a point.

"Hey!" Jim pointed to a seedy upright. Chipped black paint. It looked like something out of a speakeasy in an old movie. But cheap, very cheap.

"Well?" Jim said.

I caved in. Score another one for his mother.

On delivery day a Laurel and Hardy team in a lopsided truck drew up to our house. They used a lift to unload the piano and asked where I wanted it. Jim's mother watched.

I gave the men directions. Carry the piano to the backyard, through the outside basement door, into a laundry room, around the corner into a hallway, and set it down in the recreation room.

"Lady," said the fatter man, "we'll never get it around that corner into the recreation room."

The skinny one was more sensible. "We can cut a hole in this laundry room wall if you want," he said, "and pass the piano through."

I told them just to move it into the house and my husband would figure something out. Jim's mother took a deep breath. She looked ready to say something and didn't.

"You mean through the basement door, into the laundry room, and straight into the furnace room?" the fat one asked.

"Certainly," I said, breaking into a sweat. "My husband can cut a hole in the furnace room wall and move the piano into the recreation room from there."

I told myself not to show any weakness. Someone was taking it all in. Perhaps Amy could practice in the furnace room. Music to Read the Gas Meter By.

The two men went out to the truck and carried the piano into the backyard. I followed and Jim's mother walked behind me.

The men couldn't get the piano through the basement door. I instructed them to take the piano back up the basement steps and into the kitchen, through the dining room, through the living room, around a corner into a hallway, and into a bedroom.

The fat one began to mutter to himself. They lifted the piano, carried it up the basement steps and into the kitchen, through the dining room, through the living room, around a corner into a hallway, and set the piano down in the bedroom. HERS.

I looked the piano over. It was in better shape than I remembered it. In fact, the people at the store must have antiqued it. In fact, it wasn't the piano we bought.

The skinny fellow took it gracefully, but the chunky one increased his mutterings. The men hauled the piano back out through the living room, down the front porch steps, and into the truck.

"You broke our storm door," I said.

They spent a long time looking for the right piano to bring in. The truck contained two other pianos. Jim's mother cleared her throat. I stared her down.

They returned with the piano. It was as ugly as I had remembered it. They carried it into the house, I wrote a check, and the truck drove away.

Jim's mother didn't care for the piano in her bedroom. She let Jim know she wasn't one to complain. BUT. I said the piano stayed where it was.

Amy learned where middle C was that week. She practiced every single day from a little book her music teacher gave her. She loved to practice. Jim said his mother was getting headaches. I felt good about myself.

In two weeks our piano fell out of tune. I called a piano tuner who charged more than a plumber. He removed an old mouse nest from the piano.

"Will it play better now?" I asked.

"Not much you can do to make this thing sound better," he said, "except keep a pan filled with water in there to help with the humidity."

"You mean WATER the piano?"

"Every day," he said. "Say, where'd you pick up this thing anyway?"

I mentioned the store's name. He knew the place.

"They've gone out of business," he said.

"HA!" said Jim's mother.

IT'S O.K. REALLY

"But I tell you I live there," he yelled through the car window.

He didn't look dangerous as he pounded his fist against the glass. She raced the motor of her husband's Encore. The whirring sound leapt up to accompany the beating of her heart, pounding all out of proportion. She could only stare dumbly at him under the streetlight.

"Listen," he said. "It's all right. Just calm yourself."

She knew she should drive away. But there was a sleeping six-month-old baby inside the house. She could never leave the Lamberton child alone in possible danger like that. Suppose the shoe were on the other foot? What would she say if a frightened babysitter deserted her own children? She thought of her twin boys now safely at home, asleep in their bunk beds and her husband watching the wrestling matches on TV.

And where should she drive when she pulled away from the curb? To her house four blocks away? To the state police barracks just off the expressway? To the pay phone at the nearest 7-11 store? She didn't know what to do next. Her foot on the gas pedal trembled as she tried to steady herself.

"Look, I live in the basement of that house. They rent me a room downstairs."

"You're lying!" she shrieked. No one rented rooms in that suburban neighborhood. It was zoned for single families only. Besides, the Lambertons would have mentioned a tenant to her before they left for the movies.

"Nobody is supposed to know about it, see? It's against the law around here. They probably left in a hurry and forgot to tell you about me. Really, it's O.K."

And the worst part of it, the very worst part, was that she was all alone. After she heard the heavy footsteps coming upstairs from the basement family room, and after she flung open the front door to run to her car parked on the quiet street, she kept screaming, "There's a man in there! He broke into the house!" And not a single soul emerged from the nearby split-level houses. No one came to help. It was as if she had been abandoned on a desert isle with no one around for miles. Couldn't they hear her scream above their damned TV sets? Or did they not want to be bothered?

"Lady, I feel so sorry for you," he was saying through the closed window. "You live around here? You married? Look, drive home. Get your husband. Bring him back here. Bring anybody back. Let me explain to them. Really, it's O.K."

But the baby, the Lamberton baby. Unprotected, all alone in the house. He could kidnap the infant. Or burn the house down after he robbed it. Or God knows what all, she thought.

He reached into his pocket with a quick movement. He probably had a gun. He would shatter the plate glass with bullets and tomorrow the morning paper would read "Young Mother of Two Shot While Babysitting for Neighbors."

"I'm getting the police," she said, starting the motor.

"Wait. For Christ's sake, don't do that." He whipped out a laminated card. "Look, my name. Robert Browington Exly." He held it up. "Can you read it through the glass? Roll down the window so you can see. My picture's right here. Look."

"No." She wouldn't drive away. She should lean on the horn. That would attract attention. She fumbled, pressing all parts of the steering wheel. Where was the horn? The new Encore was the car her husband drove to work, and she had borrowed it just for that evening while her own Chevette was in the shop for repairs. Where did they put the damned horn in these cars? She strained to interpret the tiny pictures etched in white on dashboard buttons. Lights, wipers, defroster. None of them illustrated any horn.

He continued to rap on the window. "Please. At least look at my ID. I'm a systems analyst for the county. See that?"

"So?"

"Would I show you my ID if I were a criminal?"

"That picture doesn't look like you."

"They never do."

An elderly white-haired man in a paisley bathrobe appeared in the lamp-light. "Thank God you're here," the killer-rapist said. "Tell her I live in the

Lamberton house. She's the babysitter, and when I came in through the downstairs entrance, she got scared to death."

"Who?" the old man asked.

She turned off the motor so he could hear better.

The old man peered at him through thick lenses. Then he bent over to look at her behind the driver's wheel.

"Here's my ID," the killer-rapist said. "I live right there." He pointed to the house where the front door remained wide open. "That's me in this photo."

"Picture don't look like you," the old man said.

"They never do."

The old man handed him back the card and bellowed to her through the closed window. "Fellow says he rents here. But I wouldn't know. Just moved here a month ago from Tampa."

"Please come back into the house," the killer-rapist said to her. "I'll go right to my room downstairs. You won't see me for the rest of the evening. The Lambertons will be home soon. They'll tell you it's O.K. Really."

She took a deep breath. Maybe she was overreacting after all. "No," she said, much calmer now. "I'll stay in the car until they come back from the show."

"Suit yourself. Just don't call the police. O.K.?"

"O.K."

"I really understand."

"What?"

"Your fear. I really do. God, if you could only see your face." He started to move away. "Hey, I'm going in to have that beer I was about to get from the fridge when you started screaming. Want one?" He moved back to the car and pressed his forehead against the window. She noticed he had an ugly pink scar down the left side of his face. She nervously turned the ignition key and started the motor again.

"Jesus Christ," he said.

WHAT THE SEA SPITS OUT

Sharon sat hunched in the clammy kitchen and wondered if the weather in Haifa would ever turn warm enough for her to be herself again. She squashed two ants in the sugar bowl, sipped the bitter black instant coffee, opened the English-language newspaper, and turned to the business section which told how many shekels were equal to the dollar that day. The inflation went up as her own expectations came down.

She shivered in her fleece-lined jacket. There was no heater in the window-less kitchen. She felt like going back to bed and staying there until Eliahu came home from the university at five o'clock, but that would only provoke another fight. Her attention drifted away from the newspaper. Nothing registered with her except a tiny box at the bottom of one column which read "REPORT SUSPICIOUS OBJECTS."

What was on her uncrowded agenda for today? The last thing in the world she wanted to do was go sightseeing. On an earlier trip to Israel with Larry, she had worn out two pairs of walking shoes, but now she wasn't there as a tourist.

If she could force herself out of the flat, she would take a walk. But no job hunting, no, not yet. That would have to wait until she got her energy back.

From the darkness in the apartment, Sharon couldn't tell if the deceptive January sun was shining outside. "It's cool in the summer, you'll see," Eliahu said and pointed to all the bushes and trees hugging the house and bordering the shady garden in the front. "A northern exposure. My parents loved this flat for thirty-five years." But to Sharon it was just a 1930s-style garden apartment furnished heavy-handedly by an earlier generation of German Jews.

Sharon glanced at her 1984 calendar on the wall. It came from a New Jersey Savings and Loan and featured a big two-story brick colonial house with a green lawn just like the one Sharon had left behind. At home there would be snow on the ground, she thought. Seth and Mitchie would be out with their sleds in the unplowed suburban street.

She drew a sharp breath and prayed there would be no traffic. She was still their mother. Alias Madame Bovary. While Eliahu worked late last night, she huddled next to the smelly gas heater in that gloomy living room and watched a dramatization of Flaubert's masterpiece in English on Jordanian TV. She cried for Emma Bovary all the way through and wondered who was watching next door in Jordan.

Amman. Damascus. Cairo. In this Carmel neighborhood high above the harbor, the television set had perfect reception, the whole damned Middle East on tap. Last year at home she dismissed any possibility of danger with a lightness that wowed her friends. Now she worried. What if there was an air raid, and she couldn't understand where to go or what to do?

The wall phone sounded with its foreign double ring. She picked it up and hoped whoever it was spoke English. "The bomb squad was just here at the bus stop across from my building," Eliahu said. "Someone complained of an abandoned object next to the road. After they blew it up they found it was only our secretary's knitting." He laughed. Sharon didn't join in. There was a pause on the line. "We're invited to a party," Eliahu said.

"Who?"

"Shimshon. For the whole department. It's Purim next week."

"Which one is he?"

Eliahu sounded impatient. "You met him on the Carmelit. The guy with the cousin in Chicago."

She tried to recall the face they had encountered on the tiny commuter train that ran down the mountain. The Hebrew names of his colleagues sounded so much alike she couldn't tell one from the other. And she was too tired to care. The past year she had burnt herself out with the goal of breaking up her marriage to Larry. There had been arguments, hurt and farewells.

"Sure," she lied. "Costumes?"

"We'll talk about that at lunch when you come. Shimshon will join us at the Faculty Club," Eliahu said. He ended the conservation with an abrupt click.

Sharon sat motionless for a long time. Purim, my God, she thought. At the suburban temple that Larry insisted they join, religious holidays like Purim were only for the children. Once she dressed Seth as Queen Esther's uncle Mordecai. She used Larry's gold and black pajama top, a gold belt, and a fake gray beard. She won first prize. Or rather Seth did.

She glanced at the clock on the wall. Only 9:30. Time to scrub the oranges they brought from the orchard belonging to Eliahu's cousin. And then she would squeeze juice by hand to make use of the oranges because they all wouldn't fit into the small refrigerator drawer. Think small, she told herself. At first she was amazed that an ordinary American-sized load of laundry wouldn't fit into the dryer on the screened-in back porch. A good thing she wouldn't have to wash baby clothes. Neither she nor Eliahu wanted any children.

Mitchie and Seth. She felt feverish and wondered what the temperature was outside. And then she let herself think of the person she left behind for all this bliss. Larry. Mr. Holier-than-thou Larry, silently plodding away in his father's mail-order business. She wondered what kind of stepmother he would eventually bring home for their kids. Sharon rubbed some yellow liquid soap on the brush and scrubbed away at the dirt on the orange skin. Something smelled of mildew in the wooden cupboard to her right.

Song of Songs, she thought, where are you now that I need you? Larry? Who's Larry? Think Eliahu. Didn't the Bible say he was better than ten thousand other guys? Pre-eminent, it said. "His locks are curled and black as a raven." As if to fortify herself, she recited the words aloud in the freezing kitchen. "His eyes are like doves beside the water brooks, washed with milk and fitly set."

It seemed like a good idea at the time. Heidi Brotman wrote the script and asked Sharon to read a part in "The Song of Songs Revisited." And then a bunch of non-working wives, retired schoolteachers, young mothers at home with babies, whoever the Sisterhood could unearth, gave it as a reading at a Friday-evening service. Sharon, a stay-at-home mom, had nothing better to do with herself.

"This Israeli guy will liven things up a bit," Heidi said, and he did. He certainly did.

Eliahu was teaching Hebrew at the temple religious school while he finished his graduate work at the university. He was a real find and even offered to do some of the lines in Hebrew.

"For effect," Heidi said.

Sharon first noticed him when she brought her children to Sunday School. Her friends, Bev and Cheryl, discussed him while they waited for the kids to come out of class.

"Gorgeous," Cheryl said, "and he's single."

"So he says," Bev added. "If you can understand the accent."

"I'd say he's younger than us," Cheryl said. "Still in his twenties." Sharon remained silent, and when they couldn't find any other men willing to come to rehearsals, she was the one who suggested Eliahu.

She shivered again in the heatless kitchen, lit a clogged gas burner with a match, and set the kettle on the stove. Eliahu's parents owned the apartment and offered to let them live there without paying any rent. Eliahu was quick to accept without even consulting Sharon, who hadn't arrived yet from the States.

"It's completely furnished," Eliahu yelled over the phone from Haifa. "There's nothing we have to buy."

Sharon poured herself a cup of coffee. She had brought all of it on herself. After "The Song of Songs Revisited," she suggested to Eliahu that he teach an adult education class in elementary Hebrew. The group could meet at her house on Tuesday mornings. She felt restless, on the verge of getting a full-time job, or going back to school or changing her hair color.

The other women dropped out of the small class, and only Mrs. Birnbaum remained as a kind of chaperone, casting a clouded eye on Sharon as she flirted with Eliahu. When Mrs. Birnbaum left for extended cataract operations, they continued the lessons. Sharon's attempts at learning Hebrew were pitiful, but cute, he said. She prepared Chablis and tuna salad lunches. They laughed a lot together, and he teased her when she made mistakes, which was all the time.

"Madame, you are brilliant," he said. "I look at you in that sexy leotard and you dazzle me." He pronounced it "dezzle." But Sharon thought that was charming. Then she confessed to him that the Song of Songs reading was the most intellectual thing she had done since she married Larry.

"You should read it in the Hebrew," he said. "The English is nothing."

"Guess I don't have an ear for languages," she told him and he just laughed and led her into the bedroom, where Larry found them together one soap opera-ish morning in May and ordered them both in a deadly quiet voice to get the hell out.

She rinsed her cup at the scarred old-fashioned sink. The cup slipped from her fingers and broke into three parts. She really didn't care. When Eliahu's parents returned from Geneva the next year, Sharon hoped to move into a better place than this black hole.

Outside, she avoided the corner grocery shop. Eliahu left instructions for her to pick up some milk and cheese, but she felt too tired to endure the strain of trying to be understood by the elderly Polish Jewish storekeepers. They spoke the Yiddish of her Grandma Ida. Sharon didn't remember any of it. Once, at sixteen, she had a date with a boy named Gerald Ginsfarb, and Grandma Ida later commented on him.

"Speak so I can understand, Grandma," Sharon said.

"He's not the boy for you," Grandma Ida said in English. "He looks like what the sea spits out." Sharon thought that was the funniest thing she ever heard.

Her shopping would have to wait until Eliahu came with the car and drove her to the larger supermarket, where she didn't have to talk to anybody, and he could translate labels she couldn't read. Often he lost his temper about that. "You must learn some time soon," he said. Once he had read lovingly to her from the Song of Songs, "Thine head upon thee is like the Carmel . . . how fair and pleasant thou art." But the poetry worked only in New Jersey. It seemed out of place here.

Walking fast, she stuck to the same route as always, down the winding street past the old folks' home, and along the iron fence that displayed the drawings of children at the nearby school. She turned her head away from the crayoned figures. Too painful.

Sharon followed the half-broken sidewalk down a hill that led to the main street where the small shops and post office were located. She walked with long strides and brushed elderly German-speaking women who stared at her as she passed. No one else on that street walked so fast.

Sharon slowed a bit. She hated being a pedestrian, but she just couldn't get herself psyched up enough to drive. Eliahu had been quick to buy a secondhand Opel with the money Grandma Ida left in her will. He made fun of Sharon's fears and called her a coward. She was afraid she'd take a wrong turn and find herself surrounded by dark-eyed Arab children in some wild neighborhood. In Haifa it was hard to go around the block. The streets spiraled down the mountain and led you to the harbor area before you realized it. And waiting down below was the Mediterranean, all wintery gray crepe and depressing.

She hurried to the stop. If she missed the bus, she'd have to wait a whole hour for the next. It was a busy place, foul with fumes. Seated gingerly on the sheltered wooden bench, she hated what would come next. Other passengers always approached her to ask questions about routes and bus numbers in Hebrew. She would shrug and say, "I don't understand," and then they looked for someone else to ask.

That morning a harried gray-haired woman posed the inevitable question. Sharon gave her usual response. "I don't understand."

"I thought you were Israeli," the woman said in a peevish voice. Her English was quite good.

"No, American."

The woman frowned. "But you look Israeli," she insisted.

Sharon tried to be pleasant. "Sorry. I'm not."

"But surely you know some Hebrew."

"No."

"I thought all of you learn a little before you come here."

"No," Sharon answered with an idiotic smile on her face. "Not all."

"But why don't you speak Hebrew?" the woman said in an irritated voice. She did not smile back at Sharon.

"I just don't," Sharon said and amazed herself by adding, "I may be here for only a short while."

The other woman scowled, still refusing to let it go. "I thought you were Israeli. I never make that mistake."

Sharon wished the bus would hurry up and come. "No." She tried to be flippant. "Sor-ree."

The woman shrugged. She said nothing more but continued to glare at Sharon, who looked up the street toward an imaginary bus on its way.

To her left stood a green plastic trash receptacle on which someone had written in English the words "THIS IS NOT A LOVE SONG." Sharon wondered about it. It didn't make any sense. *What* was not a love song? The trash, the can, the bus stop, the stupid graffiti itself, what?

A half hour passed before Sharon's bus arrived, more crowded than usual for that time of day. She paid her fare and stood holding onto a vertical pole. In the seat opposite her sat a shabbily dressed woman with very dark eyebrows. Her right foot, bulging with bandages, was pushed out in front of her. Next to her slouched a bronzed old man with a pink and green embroidered skullcap smashed down on the back of his head. Moroccan Jews, Sharon thought.

She leaned over, watching the window for the correct street and worrying that she would pass it or get off at some similar intersection and wander around for hours. Eliahu would be furious if she missed lunch. "Can't you do anything right?" he would yell and then call her names in Hebrew, names she could only guess.

Most of all, she dreaded being lost. No, most of all she hated attracting any attention to herself. She felt that if no one noticed her, she would be considered not there, not part of her new life and not part of the old. Just whited out.

She looked down and found herself staring at the woman's foot. It was crudely wrapped, not in gauze but in ragged cloth strips torn from an old muslin sheet. The woman was tiny and dark-skinned, with the fierce eyes of a fanatic. A pale scar covered her cheek in a curved sweep like the roads leading up to Mt. Carmel.

Sharon's gaze returned to the mass of bandages just below her. Unusual shape, she thought, squared off, the bulky way it was wrapped, much too boxlike and large to contain the foot of such a small person. With great care the woman braced herself in the seat. Her narrow shoulders rose as she took a deep breath.

Watching her, Sharon felt her own knees weaken. A damp chill went through her. She glanced at the faces around her, but no one else seemed aware of the danger of those intense dark eyes. Every inch of the bus was filled. Sharon couldn't lift her arms. The strange woman's lips were moving silently as in prayer.

If she were to cry out or warn the others, Sharon thought, maybe they wouldn't understand her in time. Or maybe they would all just laugh at the cowardly American. And what if she were wrong, and they arrested the woman or did whatever they do to someone suspected of carrying a suspicious object? Or suppose there was a panic among the passengers and the driver lost control of the wheel? If anything happens to me, Sharon thought, who was there to care?

At that moment the bus lurched around a corner. Sharon lost her balance and felt herself come down hard on the bandaged toes. The woman screamed and grabbed at her foot.

"Excuse me," Sharon said and then whispered again, "I'm sorry."

But the woman wasn't letting it go at that. She continued to shriek, letting her voice rise up the scale and slide down, over and over again, full of obvious pain and pent-up rage. Her companion, the old man, took to shouting in torrents of a language Sharon didn't understand. He shook his fist in her direction. The woman never stopped screaming.

Sharon knew that everyone else on the bus was straining to see what was going on. The injured woman caught her breath and began a new round of wailing, and Sharon, after apologizing several more times, edged her way back through the other passengers standing packed in the aisle. The woman's cries penetrated to the back of the bus where Sharon could still hear them.

The vehicle swirled past a traffic island. Through the window, Sharon recognized a high, irregular stone wall near the university Faculty Club. She reached to press the buzzer, and the bus made the next stop.

Sharon pushed hard past the people blocking her way. She did not see their faces. She didn't even bother to say, "Excuse me."

EVA'S STONE

Lopsided. Ruth stared in disbelief at Eva's headstone. This year it listed to the right, one shoulder higher than the other. Forlorn, uprooted, the marker cast an untidy shadow on the grass. From the slope Ruth could look down on the gray seam of a road winding among lavender wildflowers she couldn't identify.

She leaned over with effort and brushed dust from her shoes. Not fair. Her only daughter Wendy had just this week borrowed more money for the divorce lawyer. Like mother, like daughter, both with husbands always behind in their child-support payments. Forever in need, Wendy and the two grandchildren. And now Ruth was faced with stretching her fixed income to repair this gravestone for someone who wasn't even a blood relative. Why must she worry about the long-deceased wife of her mother's brother?

A stranger. Even Ruth's mother never knew for sure if her German sister-in-law Eva was Jewish, although here she still rested more than a half century later in this Orthodox burial ground. Back then, according to tradition, Aunt Eva had to be buried at once. There was no immediate family to consult, only poor Uncle Rudy, and at that time, he himself was dying of emphysema in the hospital.

Ruth couldn't take her eyes from the humble stone that her mother had selected. Still surprisingly white, it bore the raised letters "WIFE" and "Age 44." Eva was middle-aged when she married Uncle Rudy, an aging tailor on a tiny pension. Ruth was eight years old.

"The old bachelor marries the old maid" her big sister Sylvia explained at the kitchen table as she beat a mound of sugar and egg whites for the wedding cake. Sylvia herself would remain single.

The headstone glistened in the warm September sunshine. It was the memorial time before the High Holy Days, the days of remembrance. For Ruth, the gravestones stretched out like dead marriages, no two alike. Wendy and I came to it too early, Ruth thought, Eva, too late.

That summer long ago, Rudy and Eva moved into the stuffy second-floor apartment of a city row-house and invited Ruth to visit. "I'm making my get-away," Ruthie announced, not knowing what it meant. She was giddy with anticipation as Sylvia helped her pack a battered satchel with enough clean clothes to last a week.

Ruth's family lived in three cramped rooms over their rundown grocery in a small town about twenty miles from the city. Sylvia drove them in the rusted secondhand car to Eva and Rudy's place. Then Ruth's father, taking a rare afternoon off from the store, carried the satchel to the front door and rang the bell. The white-haired landlady, Mrs. Heinrich, let them in.

"Ruthie is here!" she called out in the sharp, clean enunciation of someone American-born, unlike Aunt Eva and Uncle Rudy, who spoke with accents. But Eva had a different way of pronouncing her words, an aristocratic precision that did not sound like her husband or Ruthie's immigrant parents from Eastern Europe.

Eva and Rudy hurried down heavily waxed wooden steps. Eva kissed Ruthie and asked in her lovely low voice, "Will she be homesick?"

"If she is, I'll come and get her," Sylvia said.

"And if she's a bad girl, send her right home," Ruthie's mother said.

Eva smiled. She was fair-skinned, not dark like Ruthie's family. Eva had large bones, ample flesh to cover them, and smelled of rose water. "She is always a good girl," Eva said. "Aren't you, *mein kind?*" Everyone hugged Ruthie hard as if they'd never see her again. After they left, Uncle Rudy, no big talker, headed for the drugstore to get cigarettes and a half-pint of ice cream.

"Come," Eva said, gently taking Ruthie's hand. "I show you the dolls." She led Ruthie up the stairs to a low-ceilinged room with no windows.

It was too small for anything except perhaps a baby's crib. But there was no crib, only the mothball smell and a black steamer trunk plastered with stickers. Eva switched on a light bulb dangling from above like a white pear, took keys from the pocket of her neatly ironed cotton housedress, and opened the steamer trunk. From the blue-flowered cardboard drawers inside, she removed two porcelain Chinese coolies with gleaming orange heads and black pigtails. They sat on a garnet tray.

Eva told Ruthie she had bought the dolls in Shanghai when she worked as a traveling companion to a wealthy old woman.

"Ching Chang, Ching Chang," Ruthie said in a singsong voice as she tipped one doll toward the other. These were nothing like Ruthie's soft and cuddly baby dolls.

"Yes? You will call them Ching and Chang? I like the names you give them." Eva laughed in a contented way. "Now we put them back in the drawer. Everything in its place."

The next day Ruthie grew tired of looking at the dolls. There were no toys to play with. She wanted to slide on the slick waxed parquet floors, but Eva made her stop. The daybed where Ruthie slept reeked of camphor. She complained about everything. "You are a lucky little girl," Eva said. "Other children in this world are not so."

After Ruthie dropped Ching on the hardwood floor and chipped off his queue, Eva stopped smiling and decided Ruthie was homesick. "You will come again when you are older, yes?"

But the next summer when Uncle Rudy's breathing got so scary that he had to go to the hospital, something strange happened to Eva. She stopped scrubbing her immaculate kitchen floor. She wouldn't talk or eat. She wanted only to lie in bed and stare at the ceiling. "What can we do with her?" Ruthie's mother wept. "I have no room to keep her with us."

Ruthie visited her one last time. Mrs. Heinrich led them upstairs to an unheated bedroom, where Eva lay covered with a featherbed, and said, "Little Ruthie has come to see you." Eva never took her eyes away from the ceiling. "Ruthie," she whispered, not moving her lips. The room smelled of rose water.

Ruth hurried past Uncle Rudy's marker and returned to her parents' graves. Although she had recited the Kaddish prayer over them, she needed to ask them questions she had never wanted to face before. Why, Mama? Why did Eva get so helpless she had to be committed to the state mental hospital and die there alone? Was she upset over Uncle Rudy's illness? Or grieving over babies she never had?

Or? Or what? Ruth's mind tugged at an invisible membrane hidden deep inside her being. After Eva's death, Sylvia had found in the steamer trunk a German passport issued in 1920. It bore Eva's picture with a different name: Hedwig Lutz. Who was this Eva back then? Why did she come to America? And in a torn brown envelope Ruth's parents discovered the photograph of a helmeted Prussian officer. Who was he? A brother or a sweetheart lost in the First World War?

Ruth stared at the row of marked graves before her and let herself remember all of the horrible unmarked ones, the wartime ditches dug to hold forgotten anonymous bodies. As a child she didn't know what was going on in Germany. Kristallnacht: the night of the smashed windows, a time when all hope was burned with the holy books. Perhaps this was the unspoken cause of Eva's sickness, relatives beaten, herded into camps, murdered. Yet Ruthie could hear her mother's words sweeping like a wintry wind. "Who knows if Eva was really Jewish? I remember once when we were talking, she said Hitler had been good for Germany."

"How could a Jew have said that?" Ruthie's father demanded.

Yes, Ruth thought, but now we've read all the books, Papa. They refused to believe it could happen. Such things didn't fit into their sense of order. It was out of place. Eva's voice floated above the granite stones. "You are a lucky little girl. Other children in this world are not so."

Unanswered questions gathered in the sunshine like a swarm of gnats. Ruth straightened. I am the youngest. There is no one else left to respond. Sylvia is gone, too. Now, just me, bound to this stranger. I am her legacy. And whether she is one of us or not, whoever she may be, I'm Eva's only child, her treasured porcelain doll.

In the shade of a dying oak sat a bald young man, a blue-knit skullcap on his head. An official of the synagogue that maintained the cemetery, he balanced a clipboard on his knee.

"I want to shore up my aunt's headstone," Ruth said.

The man followed her to the spot. He leaned forward. "Died 1941," he said almost in wonder. "That's a long time ago."

"Yes," said a little girl's voice, "but I remember her."

Ruth walked with careful steps along a narrow gray road leading away from the cemetery. Next year, she must bring Wendy. On her way the old woman passed those lavender blossoms growing wild. She still didn't know what they were called, but they seemed to recognize her.

ESSAYS, LETTERS, AND ANECDOTAL WHAT-NOTS

FRANÇOISE SAGAN I WASN'T

A fair number of eternities have passed since my college graduation in 1950. Now as I look back over the years, I'm convinced it would have been easy to beat that French kid, Françoise Sagan, at her game. After all, didn't I once radiate the snobbish sangfroid of a twenty-year-old university student minoring in French? Upon getting my diploma and entering a new decade with bravado, I should have produced the very first precocious *roman démaquille* in homage to Gallic bedroom derring-do. I could have written that scandalous first novel and beaten *Bonjour Tristesse* to the punch. But it just didn't occur to me, and it's too late now. Besides, I didn't have the proper hormonal credentials.

My line of thought here may explain the ensuing Polonius to Laertes bit. As a freelancer, I hereby direct blood-sweat-and-tears advice to all writers, especially youthful zealots eager to enter a thumbs-down Colosseum. Ready? Here is the nasty truth. In the name of everything decent, *switch your field now to home economics!* (I don't hear that term used much anymore, but ask your great-grandmothers for the definition.)

No, I wasn't always such a grouch. Once editor of my university's humor magazine, I sent a droll exposé of contemporary fashions to a fancy periodical, which each year sponsored a nationwide competition for hapless coeds. The best contestants were destined to be chosen as "guest editors." In New York! The Promised Land!

The editors placed me in the top fifty finalists, but I went berserk with power and volunteered the shocking confession that I sometimes wore high heels with anklets also known as bobby sox. This was not deemed stylish in the immaculately groomed 1950s. It is the height of fashion now. Although I knew better and meant it as a joke, I was not chosen a guest editor for their September College Issue. My confidence exploded somewhere in the ionosphere and fell to earth, I know not where.

And so back in those green years, I worked in an advertising agency, married, gave birth to a couple of lively boys, and entered the Neverland of freelance writing. By the second pregnancy, I had turned "over thirty" and, consequently, could not be trusted by the flower children generation, those little pixies of the sixties. Like the rest of the world, I was too preoccupied seeking other thrills, including how to parallel park.

Below is an embalmed flashback from my early days as a clueless hausfrau living on a drab thoroughfare named for Warren G. Harding, one of our more inept presidents.

AGE OF GULLIBILITY: AN EARLY 1960S LAMENT

In a moment of homemaker ennui recently, I signed my soul away to one of those outfits that are driven to show you how much you can save on your budget if you subscribe to a half dozen fashion magazines for three years. It's rather like signing up for an army hitch during the Hundred Years' War. There's nothing one can do to keep the abominable things from arriving every thirty days. I hoped moving would help, but we were traced down by a stony-faced individual who insists he must collect $3.56 from us every three months. If we don't comply immediately, he always looks as if he's ready to cart off our warped furniture. It would serve him right.

All through this past year, I've been force-feeding myself on mindless gibberish. I'm convinced that all women's fashion magazines are expendable. A goodly number of readers despise them anyway, directing their hatred toward emaciated models who are impeccably ear-ringed, gloved, and braceleted even though the product being advertised is naught but a mundane hot-water bag.

I am a shabby suburban mother who prides herself on abstaining from 1960s high fashion. Recently, my ego was dealt a cultural blow by a slick magazine that highlighted the snobbish theme of city-girl ("The Dandies") versus country-girl ("The Dudes"). It is hard for us slobs to identify with either of them. The mink-swathed Dandies are always photographed slithering out of a limo at the Met. The Dudes wear enormously expensive cashmere sweaters with built-in hoods. They are captured grinning toothily as they pretend to look comfortable propped up by pristine haystacks.

One of my unwanted magazines, which, by the way, never bought anything from me, dedicated itself to the World of Working Women. I always thought this was very nice of them. The staff had taken upon itself the defining of "roles," which never included the Before Breakfast Laundress or the After Midnight Vacuumer. Still, an underpaid staff met deadlines with feeble attempts to make secretaries and shop clerks feel good about leaving their beds on raw January mornings. The articles did not deal with exhausted waitresses suffering from painful bunions or ladies who scrubbed the toilets at City Hall. I may have been imagining things, but it seemed to me that the editors succeeded only in burdening white-collar workers with a nasty guilt complex for not staying home with their kids.

With each issue, my lofty magazines offer menu suggestions for sophisticated homemakers. The goal is graceful living no matter what it costs, and the magnificent color photos say it all: an ecru onion leaning against the congruent triangles of amber cheese placed artfully next to a transcendently shimmering celery stalk. Although the still life sensibility could rival the best of Matisse, there never seems to be much to eat.

Certain slick fashion magazines try to dilute the blatant materialism of their ads with literary teasers, including interviews with famed scribblers. Dame Edith Sitwell's idiosyncrasies may be buried in the middle of a page touting high-waisted girdles and wired bras that promise more meaningful uplift. Oft-inebriated poet Dylan Thomas may share column space with a pitch for Kotex, featuring a perceptive drawing of a "girl named Gwen / Who is moping in bed / Though it's half-past past ten." As for fictional content, I'm convinced the obtuse short stories appearing in these flush periodicals are penned by one Seven Sister grad returning from a summer in Provence with her opulent Auntie Mame. And meanwhile, writers of my ilk are lucky to make it to a tacky hotel for a weekend in Atlantic City.

Author's addendum, 2022: If I had written a shockingly true story about a certain unnamed hotel in the above-mentioned seaside paradise, it would have been taboo for most magazines of the '50s and early '60s. The dark tale begins on the next page.

For a memorable family vacation on the Jersey shore, a casual acquaintance had recommended a tranquil retreat, reasonably priced. The place, she said, was run by two lovely old ladies, sisters from Newark. Checking in, we found one of them behind the front desk. She was anyone's dowdy grandmother. Right away she charmed my husband and me when she made a great to-do over our two small boys, patting them on their butch haircuts and offering stale Oreos.

After an educational visit to the Steel Pier, where we may have watched someone being shot out of a cannon but couldn't see well from a distance and weren't a hundred percent sure, we gobbled down Boardwalk hot dogs for dinner, guzzled orange soda, and returned exhausted to our cramped quarters. But we were not to sleep.

Throughout the night we heard heavy traffic in the hall. We heard men's voices, drunken laughter, and a woman sobbing. We heard doors banging and a cacophony of bedsprings creaking in the rooms all around us. The next day in the lobby, we passed a scowling man in a white linen suit and Panama hat. "What's them damned kids doin' in here, Grandma?" he growled at the sister of the woman who had welcomed us the day before. She shrugged. It was then my husband and I realized the awful truth. Along with our innocent little ones, ages five and seven, we had spent the night in what was once delicately called a house of ill repute.

Despite this blot on our respectability, over the years we've all remained upstanding, law-abiding citizens, and to use another archaic expression, no one is the worse for wear.

TRAILER TRAVESTY

Back in the distant year of 1968 we thought we had finally beaten the high cost of a July vacation. My thrifty husband found an ad that said, "Rent a deluxe cottage/trailer, near beaches, $75 a week. Comfortably sleeps six. Ideal for casual family fun." It seemed perfect for us and our rambunctious boys, ages eight and ten.

The hospitable host also offered campsites and campals, whatever they were. All this casual family fun was nestled in "twenty-four beautifully natural acres of pine-studded New England hills on a sparkling spring-fed lake."

In pursuit of our midsummer night's dream, we drove three hundred miles to what we hoped would be an enticing adventure. We first became doubtful when the "sparkling" lake appeared to be a gummy pond. Waiting to register in a bumper-to-bumper line, I regarded the other vehicles and their inhabitants. Each car, trailer, and camper teetered under the weight of scruffy luggage and gaggles of sunburned, itchy children, possibly studded with chigger bites.

A sweating but beaming manager, Mr. Boorke, led us up a dirt road past droopy clotheslines and lopsided picnic tables to our aluminum space capsule. The metallic door of the trailer appeared to be hermetically sealed, but Mr. Boorke forced it open with a big smile on his face as if to say this was all part of casual family fun. Inside the trailer/cottage, he showed us how to convert the breakfast nook into what he called "additional roomy sleeping quarters."

"You probably won't need it," he said as our two sons climbed into an upper Pullman-like berth and began some serious wrestling. "Your bunk beds are full-sized double beds."

It took a while to unpack, and we all turned grouchy looking for a place for everything while we tried to put everything in its place. Even in our own six-room home, our family has never been overly qualified at playing the neatness game.

"This is what I thought we were taking a vacation *from*," I said. "There's no space for a garbage bag unless we hang it from the ceiling."

The linoleum floor was gritty with sand, unusual because we were twenty-five miles away from the nearest beach. It could have been gravel tracked in from a neighboring construction site we had passed on the road. By very late afternoon, we were minimally settled in our digs, cooled only by nonexistent New England breezes.

On the verge of a complete meltdown, I abandoned husband and children to sit in our car for a few minutes of much-needed isolation from reality. Although I ran the motor and switched on the newly installed air-conditioning system (a separate unit that did not come with the automobile), there was no respite from the record-breaking humidity. The crackling ashen sky heralded the possibility of a storm with an abundance of lightning. All adults and their hordes of children were doomed, trailer-trapped for the evening. I noted that someone had strung empty cardboard milk cartons festively from tree to tree in preparation for a party that was not to be.

Hours later, in competition with the moon and stars overhead, our woodland community became eerily illuminated. All night long, cars and trailers rumbled by, flashing their headlights into our rustic retreat.

Bedtime itself provided a challenge. "They call this a double bed?" my husband muttered from our lower berth. On their higher plane, the boys had exhausted themselves in a regimen of routine jabs and discreet punches.

"The brochure said it comfortably sleeps two," I said.

"Sleeps two WHAT?" he snarled as he arose to convert the breakfast nook into a cot for himself. We had packed only enough blankets for two beds. He had to cover himself with a plastic tablecloth.

Happily, the shower didn't work, no problem as far as our sons were concerned. The next day we endured more suffering from the effects of Mr. Boorke's false advertising. There was a price to pay for renting such deluxe digs. We were to learn that a certain Hatfield-McCoy feud existed between the trailer/cottage plutocrats and the proletarian tent-dwellers from the other side of the tracks. Near the sparkling lake.

After a few days of adjusting to life in mosquito-dominated splendor, my husband reluctantly took one of his newfound buddies on a grand tour of our luxurious showplace.

"Just want to see how the other half lives," said the scruffy old gentleman, a diehard camper of the old school.

Our sons made themselves scarce by climbing into their beds, and I inhaled myself into the breakfast nook. The visitor eyed our foot-wide sink, turned on the faucet, and sniffed with disdain. "You folks call this camping out? Hot running water?"

"The shower is broken," I said hopefully.

He touched our mattresses. "Beds!" he snorted. "We sleep on the ground."

My husband had an answer for that. "Yeah? Well, I sleep on the kitchen table."

Our guest shook my husband's hand warmly. "You've got me there, pal," he said.

Note: In the fifty-four years that have passed since then, we have not gone back. The possibility of a return appears slim as time dashes by.

WORDS UNSPOKEN

In more than eighty years as a published poet, journalist, advertising copywriter, and editor, I find among my souvenirs an accumulation of plaques and merit certificates, even a 1998 Courage Award from the Dystonia Medical Research Foundation. It happens to be my favorite because it is a trophy that recognizes not the imagination but reality.

In 1995 after writing *Ladies First: Rhymes and Times of the Presidents' Wives and Other Female Fantasies*, it was my own fantasy to transform the poems into a musical stage production since I could no longer do public readings. My dream came true, and for ten years we took our show to community colleges, churches, and civic groups as well as retirement complexes and nursing homes. Often when we performed for the elderly and the ill, at the conclusion of the performance I made a point of chatting with each member of the audience. Although it was a great effort for me to produce audible speech, I had an opportunity to meet those who were recuperating from strokes or laryngectomies. Sick as they were, they managed to say how much they enjoyed the performance. My own problems shrank in comparison. I felt humble and fortunate.

This is what I've learned. We must become regenerated into a broader personal image of ourselves. My voice was always who I was. When tests at the National Institutes of Health revealed abductor spasmodic dysphonia, I felt my whole being was reduced to the raspy whisper issuing from my mouth. I've learned we must integrate our losses into the whole of what we are, recognizing that we are larger and much more powerful than the part of us that has undergone change.

Our imagination can help us adjust to reality, but first it's important to acknowledge what has happened to us and to put our vanity into its proper place. Then, not looking back, we must conjure up magic ways to vanquish the dragon.

I do not forget that once upon a time I had a voice that went everywhere with me. I thought my voice and my soul were one and the same, but they weren't. A time came when the voice evaporated into the air and was almost gone. Then something else flew in to take its place.

It was an intangible spirit, an inner voice as constant as the hum of a bee. It grew in intensity until it became a shout and then a roar and commanded me not to dwell on what had vanished into the mist, what was lost, what I couldn't do. It spelled out my course clearly like an actor's directions in a play script, telling me to forget the previous roles I had played and make the most of the one I have now, discover something new about it each day, and test the limits of what I can become.

It has grown to be a hundred times bigger than my original voice ever was.

A PREDICTION

One day literary sleuths researching defunct magazines of the twentieth century will unearth a definitive kind of quotidian poetry. It may be as short as a couplet here, a quatrain there, about the futility of cutting crabgrass or an endless wait in a dentist's office or a well-meant suburban cookout gone bad. My point is this. When such clear and honest writing reflects the mundane strife of ordinary people, why shouldn't such light verse bear a more scholarly label? Why not call it what it is: Contemporary American Folk Poetry.

With the disappearance of print magazines and newspapers, these rhyming crumbs of day-to-day living are sadly missing in the twenty-first century. The future will take a good, hard look at them, I am certain. The future has a knack for doing that.

Consider the output of Dorothy Parker, whose light verse appeared in the *New Yorker*, *Vanity Fair*, *American Mercury*, and other national periodicals of her day. Much of her work we could tag as contemporary folk poetry, written in the voice of her time, including often-quoted wisecracks that rang a bell with reasonably educated Americans. Thanks to Mrs. Parker, everyone knew that men didn't make passes at girls who wore spectacles on their noses.

Her lines burst with the daily cares of a cosmopolitan woman partially free from the restraints that existed for most women of her time. She is never completely released from the control of men. The poem "Chant for Dark Hours" bewails the self-serving distractions of the male gender while females must juggle their schedules accordingly. "Some men," she complains, "some men / cannot pass a / Crap game" or resist a bar-room or a golf course. Or even a stop at a haberdasher's. Meanwhile, Dorothy writes, women must wait, pass the time hanging in limbo, and they are advised to "Read a book, and sew a seam, and slumber if you can." And the rueful punchline: "All your life you wait around for some damn man!" Women can still identify with that. Yes, numerous men may argue that the concluding summation can apply to tardy females, and they're right, but it doesn't scan, and how many words rhyme with "woman"?

Parker's legacy, a perfect example of urban folk poetry composed in the 1920s, '30s, '40s, and '50s, reflects the impatience of worldly-wise, city women griping about the frustrations of their day. The organized feminism of the 1970s is still decades away. Her language is often dated, but that lends historical heft. Although certain slightly mildewed expressions may need refreshing, the wisdom is timeless.

In the lines quoted above, the wayward boyfriend is distracted by a "barroom," a quaint term recalling for me a more serious poem, "The Face on the Bar-Room Floor." I doubt that this nineteenth-century tearjerker by H. Antoine D'Arcy influenced Parker's verse in any way, and anyway, it's too late to ask her. She also suggests that her gentleman friend may have been delayed by a stop at the haberdasher's, a word unknown to anyone born after the 1960s. Today "haberdasher" is an obsolescent mouthful spoken possibly by my own fading generation, who may remember that President Harry Truman once worked at such an establishment, selling shirts, pants, and BVDs in Kansas City.

If anyone cares, be assured there is pure gold to be discovered in the light verse of the past century. Ignore the few odious odes; explore the humorous wordplay of Richard Armour, Ogden Nash, Morris Bishop, David McCord, Phyllis McGinley, Helen Bevington, Arthur Guiterman, and Margaret Fishback. They wrote brilliant filler for the best magazines and newspapers in the country. Let the record show that their work will one day be ripe for scholarly dissertations on Contemporary American Folk Poetry. Seminars will be held. Doctorate degrees will flourish. Students will deconstruct in all directions and establish academic societies devoted to furthering the existential influences of light iambic pentameter.

Mark my prophetic words, and pray for battered bards everywhere.

THE VOICE LESSON

Bontsha Schweig is my folk hero. This silent man, a creation of the Yiddish writer I. L. Peretz, is my role model, the perfect mentor. We are soul mates because a funny thing happened to me on the way to grandmotherhood. The muscles that control my vocal cords fell into disrepair, and not all the doctors in the world could determine the cause or find a cure. I know because my search for help took me to just about every physician in the book.

That said, why should I identify with Bontsha? Well, if you recall the story, he was a humble, reticent man who never asked for anything, never once raised his voice in anger at the curve balls his pitiful life had tossed him. When he entered Paradise and the compassionate angels told him he could have whatever he desired, he asked for just one thing. In Hilde Abel's translation of this story, found in *A Treasury of Yiddish Stories*, he requested only "a hot roll with fresh butter."

Although I like the idea of a quiet Jew, isn't that description an oxymoron? How can any Jew be quiet? Jews were created to communicate the message from Mt. Sinai. We were always in voice, the cable news network of mankind, a verbal bridge to the worlds of religion, philosophy, literature, and science. We gave civilization a code of conduct grounded in words. And although our stuttering teacher Moses wasn't exactly a desirable after-dinner speaker, he telegraphed his intentions well enough to lead us out of Egypt through the wilderness to Canaan.

The doctors I consulted did come up with a handy name for my malady: spasmodic dysphonia. And just as Ecclesiastes explains that "of making books there is no end," so it is with labeling. All things these days have ponderous labels. In my case, it creates a problem. Imagine, seven whole syllables to answer the inevitable question, "What's wrong with your voice?" Whoever invented that label created a real obstacle for persons with voice disorders. The words "spasmodic dysphonia" don't come easily, even to the silver-tongued.

With the best intentions the Creator of the Universe began the trend by telling Adam to label all living creatures, but somehow, over the millennia, labels have become pretentious and at worst can scare you with whatever is behind them, real or imaginary. I have learned not to let my knees buckle at pompous, clinical nomenclature. A label itself shouldn't be intimidating. Sometimes if the medicine men can't cure us, we must choose a different route. Back in the 1980s when the SD treatment of choice, Botox injections, did not work for me, I came to one harsh conclusion: put up and shut up.

For solace I looked to my tribe, that extended and original *mishpachah*, my family of heroes and heroines from the Jewish tradition. On days when the abductor muscle controlling my larynx produces a raspy whisper or doesn't work at all, I think of barren Hannah, wife of Elkanah, in the Bible. As she prayed to conceive a child, only Hannah's lips moved; her voice could not be heard. Eli, the priest, thought she had been hitting the bottle, all that muttering to herself and no recognizable sound coming out. But, voice or no voice, the Almighty welcomed her prayer and answered it.

From this story, I have learned that although the Sh'ma ("Hear O Israel, the Lord our God, the Lord is One") may soundlessly issue from my mouth while everyone else is saying it out loud, the conviction I hold is as strong as any in the congregation. Audible speech isn't necessary to get through to our Creator, who, among other things, is also a good listener.

A favorite part of synagogue services for me has always been the Shemoneh Esrei, the Silent Prayer. Here everyone has an equal chance. In the vast quiet of standing co-worshippers, I become philosophical and consider the role of silence in Judaism. Every year during the High Holy Days, I locate this favorite sentence: "The preparation of the heart is the concern of man, but speech is the gift of the Lord," and I am thankful for that gift on those days when my still small voice delivers.

Although SD is not a life-threatening condition, it can be cruel. Sometimes it will respond to the therapy of the speech pathologist, and sometimes not at all. I'm grateful whenever it does and keep cool on bad days, especially when persons with hearing problems grow edgy with me. Still, I recall with pleasure that famous *Seinfeld* TV episode about the Low Talker. No one laughed louder than I did.

In free moments I search for references to speech or lack of it in holy passages. The Book of Job offers this marvelous line: "Days should speak and multitude of years show wisdom." If our days speak well for us, it means we are eloquent in good deeds. The Book of Proverbs also tells us, "The wise in heart will accept commandments, but a babbling fool will fall." There are plenty of babbling fools around these days, but as another ancient proverb proclaims, "In much talk, transgression is not lacking, but one who restrains his [or her] lips is wise."

When we give thanks in prayer, I express appreciation that if spasmodic dysphonia happens, better it should affect a writer like me than a teacher, a cantor, or heaven forbid, an Israeli tour guide. If the computer isn't down, I can always get my message out. On those occasions that require me to contribute to a discussion or speak on the phone, I plan ahead on paper, edit my words carefully, breathe from the diaphragm, and pray not to run out of sound too soon. Writing poetry has trained me to whittle thoughts down to the core.

I study under the best of teachers. From the gentle Bontsha I learn humility; Hannah schools me in the efficacy of silent prayer. And each Passover the disfluent but persevering Moses inspires me to let my actions do the talking. The role models speak volumes.

HELLO, YOUNG WRITERS OR
WHATEVER YOU ARE

You ask me how to be a writer, and I am foolhardy enough to answer. Or try. There is no manual that goes with the job. A writer just grows into things. You learn as you go, and the creative process is anything but romantic.

For me, dry research often opens the doors. Or I may see a quote in a newspaper or an article about odd human behavior, and it will trigger off something. On particularly barren days I read history or autobiography for motivation and mental adrenalin. Sometimes it's an assignment thought up by a desperate editor, and I simply root around in my imagination for facts, images, pictures, and wordplay that can be used to enlarge upon the initial idea. I use whatever is in my files and never ever throw anything out. The people around me supply their faces, personalities, and philosophies to draw upon. Everything is fair game.

You ask me what are the challenges and rewards? If you have to ask, perhaps you should become a claims adjuster or a chocolate dipper. Each writer has her own bête noir to battle. I do. I am not one thing or the other. I am a light verse poet who also writes serious poetry. I am a journalist who produces fiction and plays. But often I've produced things that are not suitable for mass publications, and that's when those somewhat snooty "little" magazines who call themselves "literary" come into play. My challenge is to work with blinders in one field at a time and avoid mixing it all up however great the temptation.

The most satisfying reward for me is discovering strangers who have read my work. The next best reward? Finishing whatever I've started and finding a hospitable home for it. One of the most delightful things is to start from scratch with no ideas in my head and whack at the bushes until some wobbly little concept emerges, puts on some poundage, and finally, swallows me up, computer and all.

You ask me to comment on a career in writing. That's a vague phrase. What kind of writing? How do you define career? I've learned from years of experience that it's easier to find work doing PR puff pieces or to grind out gobbledygook for a government agency or to edit a trade magazine than it is to publish a novel, have a play produced on Broadway, or create a prime-time sitcom. It's easier to launch a newsletter for a nonprofit group than to sell short stories to the *New Yorker*. But you knew that.

If you want to write and aren't proud, you can still find opportunities. The competition for the lesser jobs is keen, and the pay may be peanuts. If a beginner perseveres, she can make a career in a nonliterary writing field. Those who see themselves as Virginia Woolf or Emily Brontë are headed for heartache. And a pox on the dilettantes who would rather daydream about living the glamorous life of a promiscuous novelist in a picturesque cottage on a windswept hill, or flighty types who chatter incessantly about all the incredible short stories they will tackle one day. These jokers are wasting their time and yours. Avoid them.

The crisis for writers lies not in unearthing ideas or putting one word after another in acceptable fashion. The crisis is finding People Who Read. Most Americans don't, and many of the younger ones can't. The whole world of writers and readers is in turmoil now, and while cyberspace may be a marvel, it could very well be our destruction as professional writers. Don't let it happen.

In the meantime, go ahead and write if that's what you want to do. Venture forth even if it's nothing more dramatic than editing a club newsletter. Take what you can find and keep an eye open for something better. Read good literature. Go for long walks. Listen to classical music.

Become aware of creativity other than your own. Learn something about art and music, past and present. Read history, biographies, bone up on geography. If you prefer a peer group looking over your shoulder as you write, sign up, and feel free to jump ship when you feel like it.

One thing more. Experienced writers who survive physically and mentally share this creed: be able to laugh at it all and say, "To hell with it!" even if you don't mean it. Never assemble all eggs in one basket. Markets change and disappear, editors lose their jobs or die, original work is plagiarized every day.

Do you still want to be a writer? OK. Be ready for rejection no matter how old or how young you are. Or how brilliant. When minor triumphs come your way, savor them. You're lucky to find a few delicious crumbs. Others aren't even that fortunate. And if, on the chance that you somehow score big, don't let it get in the way of remaining a human being. Either way, it's important for writers of all genders to reserve chunks of time for parents, husbands, children, lovers, and friends. After all, a dark PC monitor is not much of a companion when you have whatever virus is fashionable these days.

SIGNATURES, WRIT BY HAND

Some people fatten their autograph collections by hanging around stage doors and making pests of themselves or stalking Capitol Hill when Congress is in session.

A shrinking violet myself, I prefer to grow my own autograph collection organically, hoarding replies from famous people to whom I've written pseudo-serious letters. That way, even if I do get on someone's nerves, I'm not around to witness it.

Washington, D.C., might seem an autograph-hunter's Eden: all those celebrity pols! The trick is pinning them down. Even the letter ruse isn't certain. The autopen, popular with politicians since the early '60s, reproduces signatures with amazing faithfulness. Experts suggest you fit one signature over another; if they're identical, they weren't signed by hand. Still, I claim an authentic Spiro Agnew, signed when he was still governor of Maryland.

If you favor political signatures, election year may be the time to begin a collection. Candidates are never more accessible—and since you can't predict the winner, take anything you can get. Rallies and fundraising dinners are good places to seek. And ye shall find.

Some autograph-hunters are shameless and relentless. The *Wall Street Journal* once featured a Good Humor truck driver in Brooklyn who spent eighteen years collecting ten thousand signatures of Broadway performers, garnering sometimes twenty-five new ones each day. That's a lot of Popsicles.

Autograph collecting goes back to Roman times—Julius Caesar's day, although on the Ides of March nobody thought to ask for his signature. The Bard himself left only six known copies of his signature, "Shaksper," according to sources at the Folger Shakespeare Library. Sixteenth-century German, Dutch, and Belgian students collected their friends' autographs in small albums known as *alba amicorum*. Victorian young ladies swooned all over themselves to capture the genuine scrawl of Charles Dickens, a collector's item to be cherished forever in their dainty ribbon-bound books.

Poets were also in great demand among early autograph hounds. Today, I doubt that an Allen Ginsberg signature is valued anywhere near as much as a Tom Cruise or a Max Scherzer. Heroes change. But back in the 1800s, people cannibalized letters solely for the autographs; only the signatures wound up pasted in albums.

My interest sprouted from an ancient red volume, six inches by four, that I received on my twelfth birthday. In addition to signatures of my parents and siblings, the book brims over with the rhymed prepuberty sentiments of my young classmates.

The little verses they wrote could serve as models for Washington celebrities signing autograph books—for example, "Way back here / Out of sight / I write my name / Just for spite . . . Richard Nixon."

Or, "There are silver ships, / And there are gold ships / But there is no ship / Like a Chairmanship . . . Your Congressman."

Or, how about: "I luv ya, I luv ya / I luv ya so well / If I had a peanut / I'd give you the shell . . . Jimmy Carter."

For serious collectors, there are excellent books on what to look for and how to interpret abbreviations like ALS (autograph letter signed) and AMsS (autograph manuscript signed). By subscription, auction houses may provide valuable catalogues. Check out the quarterly journal *Manuscripts* as well as *The Collector*, a magazine for autograph and historical collectors. Don't count on getting rich. Unless you're already worth megabucks, there's no way you'll ever get your hands on an original Shaksper or a signer of the Declaration of Independence.

But to secure Grandma's handwriting for posterity or little Megan's nursery-school scribble-scrabble, I heartily recommend keeping a family autograph book. And if you want to squirrel away a cocktail napkin bearing the moniker of George Plimpton or an auto-penned letter blessed by Hillary Clinton, go ahead. In a hundred years, who knows what it will be worth? (Want to trade a Zbig Brzezinski for a slightly worn Spiro Agnew?)

TO THE EDITOR

Gazette, April 1991

"A Life in Shoe Biz" was one of your best articles. The excellent writing evoked memories—the sights, smells, and mystique of the old-time shoe repair shop. It was that kind of place where I grew up, playing underfoot. Excuse the pun.

Pop, a cobbler trained by his shoemaker father in Lithuania, owned the same kinds of venerable tools and machinery as the men in your story. I remember the finisher, the stitcher, the steel last. Sometimes we kids pretended his shop was a medieval torture chamber.

There were Cat's Paw rubber heels in red boxes, the only bright color in a drab black and brown landscape. The floor was littered with leather dust shaved from amber slabs of leather. The dust had a sharp, acrid smell and the consistency of sawdust. In winter my father scattered it on the front sidewalk to keep potential customers from falling on the icy pavement and suing us into oblivion.

Most touching of all was your reporter's description of the battered hands. Pop had once driven a tack far under his left thumb fingernail, and the black mark remained there like a shoemaker's badge of honor. With fingers raked raw, he ripped away mammoth black rubber heels from farmers' work shoes to which the smell of fresh manure still clung.

Although the gentlemen are Italian in your story, Pop was an Eastern European Jew. But each month he received a free trade magazine called *Il Calzolaio*, which he figured meant "shoemaker." Not knowing a word of Italian, he studied the pictures of shoe repair shop owners in faraway cities as if these unknown artisans were kinfolk. Unfortunately, he and I never understood any cartoon captions in the magazine.

Your article also triggered off memories of his favorite 1940s Griffin Shoe

Polish radio spot in which an anonymous ad writer rose to the heights of lyricism with a singing commercial called "Time to Shine." (Memorable line: "Some folks aren't particular how they look about the feet. If you wore shoes upon your head, you'd be sure that they were neat.") Thanks for a great story.

TO THE EDITOR

Gazette, April 1990

I never saw anything like it. After last weekend's unwelcome spring snowfall, I was engaged in a wintery Sunday morning constitutional through my College Gardens neighborhood.

Undaunted, I dodged the snow falling from the flowering trees, which reacted to the storm like beauties who had just had their hair done at an expensive shop before taking a disastrous pratfall into a snowbank.

All at once, on the messy wet sidewalk before me, a suicidal robin appeared. It had given up trying to distinguish the white blobs of snow from the fallen white petals on the grass. Flat-footed, the bird walked in front of me without even bothering to flee from my approaching Brooks athletic shoes.

I had never met such a down-in-the-bill fowl in my entire life. Although I was close enough to step on its tail, it just didn't give a damn any more. Feeling guilty, I hoped it didn't recognize me as a member of a local civic commission, which a few years ago sponsored an essay contest for public school children. It resulted in the election of the robin to a high public office with an impressive title.

Bedraggled, depressed, badly in need of counseling, the robin turned to me as if to say, "Is this any way to treat the Official Bird of Montgomery County? Next time don't do us any favors!"

TO THE EDITOR

Washington Post, October 2012

In your article "Could politics use a bit of wisdom from the Mad Men?," an advertising executive bemoaned the failure of campaign advertising to come up with fresh ideas. He complained that the people in charge are afraid of abandoning techniques that worked previously. How about their penchant for duplicating ideas that didn't work?

Six decades ago, I was a callow intern in the media department of an influential East Coast agency. We managed to snare the Adlai Stevenson presidential campaign in 1952, a real coup because it gave our New York and Baltimore account executives a chance to use television for the first time in a presidential campaign. Our crew of unshaven, sweaty copywriters, who in no way resembled the oversexed 1960 studs of "Mad Men," were convinced that a sensible, jingle-inspired song would carry us to victory over a wishy-washy opponent, a man named Dwight Eisenhower, who had a hard time deciding whether he was a Republican. Our guys came up with a masterpiece called "Don't Let 'Em Take It Away!"

Last night, sixty years later, this Democrat watched in horror as a TV commercial listed the poor track record of the Republican Party and ended with the ominous statement, referring to Medicare and Social Security benefits, "Don't let Mitt Romney take them away!" If nothing succeeds like success and everything fails like failure, I think I'll move to one of those newly discovered planets in the cosmos.

MINUTES TO REMEMBER

Author's note: What a distinct honor it was for this child of immigrants to participate in a twentieth-century celebration marking the 1787 birth of the United States Constitution! With local government support and priceless Historical Society documentation, I wrote the following commemorative fragments to be read aloud at official weekly sessions of county legislators during the summer of 1987.

June 9. Two hundred years ago today the Constitutional Convention in Philadelphia had already been under way for more than two weeks. And Maryland's delegates were on the job! They had been officially chosen in Annapolis on May 26, one day after the Convention started. Although delegate nominations had been made in April 1787 by the Maryland state legislature, some nominees had declined. The chosen delegates, who some critics said were "second string," nevertheless had either served in Congress or held state offices and included James McHenry, Luther Martin, John Frances Mercer, Daniel of St. Thomas Jenifer, and Montgomery County's Daniel Carroll. More about them all between now and September 17 in our exclusive County Council Constitutional Minutes.

June 16. By June 16 a battle royal was raging at the Constitutional Convention over Madison's Virginia Plan. Quick agreement was given to having three branches of government and a bicameral legislature. But then the delegates began to cluster into two warring camps: the Federalists, who favored a strong central government, and the Nationalists, who wanted to continue a loose federation of states with only minor changes. Our feisty Maryland delegation was split down the middle. But Montgomery's pride, Daniel Carroll, a champion of strengthening the central government over the power of the individual states, was on the side of the angels. More next week in our Constitutional Minute.

June 30. Two hundred years ago today, the gentlemen at the Constitutional Convention in Philadelphia were sizzling under their wigs in a heated debate over a question that directly affected Maryland's future. Tempers flared as the temperature soared. Perhaps an exasperated delegate might well have scribbled on a scrap of parchment the following poetic lines:

> *The little states are much upset;*
> *They fear the mammoths will forget*
> *A Maryland or a Delaware*
> *Deserve their legislative share.*
> *Should size on map or population*
> *Determine who will rule this nation?*
> *If such is what this pact will bring*
> *My Maryland won't sign the thing!*

And so the battle lines were clearly drawn. As Ben Franklin put it, with proportional representation, the smaller states "feared their liberties would be in danger," and with equality of votes, the larger states "felt their money would be in danger." Who would win the battle? More in our upcoming Constitutional Minutes.

July 7. It was two hundred years ago this Thursday, that Montgomery County's own Daniel Carroll of Rock Creek took his seat at the Constitutional Convention. The distinguished owner of an estate in what is now the Forest Glen area, Daniel Carroll brought with him a wealth of experience as a seasoned civil servant. He had signed the Articles of Confederation and had served as president of the Maryland State Senate and as a delegate to Congress. Daniel was accustomed to the sound of gentlemen's voices raised in rough-and-tumble debate. He had arrived amid a battle royal over a committee report on state representation. The resulting Compromise provided for a House of Representatives elected on the basis of population and a Senate in which each state would have an equal vote, a recommendation much desired by Maryland. To appease the larger states, a special clause was inserted that only the lower house could originate money bills without the State's having any power to change them. And with Daniel Carroll now on hand, the Federalists' team was considerably strengthened in the tug of war with those who desired to keep the loose federation of states. More next time in our Constitutional Minute.

July 21. On this day two centuries ago the Constitutional Convention argued long and hard over what shape the Judicial Branch of our government should take. Let us permit the good gentlemen their arguments and withdraw from the stifling heat of Philadelphia to the cool waters of Rock Creek in Montgomery County and to Joseph Park, an estate in the Forest Glen area. Here Eleanor Carroll, mother of our delegate to the Convention, sits in a darkened room and thinks of her son Daniel, whose birthday will be tomorrow, July 22. Eleanor, now eighty-three years old, is an educated woman with a deep respect for learning. Immersed in memories of her son's service to Maryland, she recalls how she sent him far away from home to a Jesuit college in Flanders for his education. It was the same school she chose for his brother John, destined to become the first Catholic bishop in the United States. Her two sons fill her with great joy. The old woman's lips move silently as she says her rosary and prays for her son Daniel and the fruitful outcome of his Philadelphia meeting. And today we all join her in wishing Daniel Carroll a happy 257th birthday. Additional historical Minutes to come next week.

July 28. Two hundred years ago today the men of the Constitutional Convention took a breather during a much-needed ten-day recess. Meanwhile, the Committee on Detail prepared a draft constitution from the resolutions already agreed upon. Included was the Great Compromise, providing for a House of Representatives elected on the basis of population and a Senate in which each state would have an equal vote. It had been a supreme victory for Daniel Carroll and others from the smaller states. What's more, the Convention had voted thumbs down on a proposal to give both the Judicial and the Executive branches the right to veto national and state laws. The delegates had also thrown out a proposal that would allow Congress to override state laws. Most important, the framers of the Constitution had ruled that the acts of Congress and all treaties should be the supreme law of the several states, and the Supreme Court's jurisdiction should extend to all cases arising under laws passed by Congress.

Now after two months of being cooped up in oven-like temperatures, the delegates may well have agreed with the wag who said, "The heat was so dreadful here that I found there was nothing left for it but to take off my flesh and sit in my bones." More of our Constitutional Minutes next time . . . after the cranky gentlemen have cooled off a bit.

August 4. During the dog days of August two hundred years ago, the Constitutional Convention was rocked with explosive debate on slavery and the slave trade. Here in Montgomery County slaveowners were directly affected by a Convention compromise which postponed prohibition of slave importation until 1800. A further concession extended the end of slave trading to 1808. Delegate Daniel Carroll himself kept fifty-three slaves, the second largest number owned by anyone in the county. But the scourge of involuntary human bondage was not so widespread here as elsewhere in Maryland. Charles Carroll of Carrollton, Daniel's distant cousin, who signed the Declaration of Independence, owned the most slaves in the state, numbering over three hundred. In deciding how Maryland's population would be counted for representation and taxation, the founding fathers came up with the "Three-Fifths Compromise," counting five slaves equivalent to three free persons. It was outrageously unfair but acceptable to these men of their time, men who did not foresee that the unresolved issue of slavery would in the next century launch a bloody civil war, ripping apart the perfect Union they labored so hard to create. Stay tuned for our next Constitutional Minute.

September 15. Two hundred years ago today the final draft of the Constitution was approved, and thirty-nine weary gentlemen heaved a collective sigh of relief. Of the original five Maryland delegates, three remained to sign the document on September 17: Daniel of St. Thomas Jenifer, James McHenry, and Montgomery County's Daniel Carroll. Their Anti-Federalist colleague, Luther Martin, the feisty attorney general of Maryland, had already left Philadelphia, determined to rally forces against ratification. Martin feared the states were vulnerable to the "potential aggression of a centralized government." Meanwhile,

Daniel Carroll, who signed his public letters "A Friend to the Constitution," would return home to take his fight to the people.

In a rough and tumble county election of State Convention delegates to ratify the Constitution, Carroll's Federalists carried Montgomery County by nearly three to one. The Anti-Federalists of Maryland fought tooth and nail at the State Convention. Luther Martin even talked himself into laryngitis. But on April 28, 1788, Maryland ratified the Constitution by a vote of 63 to 11. And later Daniel Carroll, a Catholic whose family had known religious discrimination, would spearhead the drive for the First Amendment on religious liberty in the Bill of Rights. Surely Carroll would have applauded the words of a noted twentieth-century statesman, who said, "Liberty does not consist in mere declaration of the rights of men. It consists in the translation of those declarations into definite actions."

Our venerable document endures. Long live the U.S. Constitution!

ACKNOWLEDGMENTS

"Superfrog," published in *The Pen Woman* in 1995, was the national first-prize winner in the 1994 Biennial adult short story competition sponsored by the National League of American Pen Women (NLAPW). The following stories appeared in *Chesapeake*, a regional NLAPW literary magazine edited by Marta Knobloch and Vonnie Crist: "Piano Blues" (1993), "It's O.K. Really" (1995), and "Eva's Stone" (1996, originally titled "Amelia's Stone"). "Signatures, Writ by Hand" (1980) appeared in the *Washington Post* Weekend Section; "The Voice Lesson" (1998) in *New Light* magazine of Temple Israel, Great Neck, New York; "Hello, Young Writers or Whatever You Are" (1996), prize-winning essay in NLAPW's national Biennial contest; "Words Unspoken," 1997 Courage Award, with excerpted paragraphs appearing in an autobiographical article (1998) in the Dystonia Medical Research Foundation's outstanding magazine *Dystonia Dialogue*; and "Constitutional Minutes" (1997), published by Montgomery County (MD) County Council and Montgomery Historical Society. Deepest gratitude to Len for all his efforts in solving the technical and editorial problems of a nonagenarian, and thanks for the loving encouragement of Joe, Dina, Cynthia, Isaac, Amy, Mira, and Ezra. Kudos to Kathleen Mills and Carolyn K. Lewis for expert editing and book design.

ABOUT THE AUTHOR

In her ninety-plus years, Mollee Kruger has done just about every kind of writing except skywriting, which, for carbon footprint reasons, she avoids. Born in Bel Air, Maryland, six months before the start of the Great Depression, the veteran author has labored at her craft for more than eight decades. When she was twelve, her first published poem appeared in the *Aegis*, a local newspaper. By seventeen, she had become a paid columnist for the weekly *Harford Gazette*. She won a top award for light verse in a *Scholastic* magazine competition, and while still a teenager, sold a humorous poem to *Woman's Home Companion*, a national periodical. During the years before acquiring a Bachelor of Arts degree in English at the University of Maryland, she worked as managing editor of the campus magazine and also wrote a prize-winning essay on college life for *Mademoiselle* magazine.

Since then, Kruger has received numerous national and regional awards for serious, humorous, and inspirational poetry, essays, and short stories. She wrote a weekly syndicated newspaper column of light verse for twenty years and collaborated with composers and choreographers who set her poetry to music and dance. At the beginning of the twenty-first century, she received an award for achievement in the humanities, and in 2003 the University of Maryland, her alma mater, included her papers in its holdings of literary manuscripts and letters.

Married for fifty-eight years to the late internationally recognized scientist Jerome Kruger, she has two sons, two daughters-in-law, and two grandchildren. She has lived in Rockville, Maryland, for the past half century. Following publication of her recent memoir, *Port of Call*, Mollee Kruger has spent the past two years on *A Collector's Item*, her twelfth book. The author agrees with the French novelist Stendhal, who wrote in his memoir, "Without work, the vessel of life has no ballast."